SHADY AFFAIRS AT SPRUCE-JUNGLE

An Aventurous Suspense Love Story

M K Sumangala

I dedicate this book to all my passionate readers, my parents, my family and friends
LOVE YOU ALL FOR YOUR VALUABLE SUPPORT AND ENCOURAGEMENT

Copyright © February 2021 Sumangala M Kadi

All rights reserved

The characters and events portrayed in this book are fictitious. Any similarity to real persons, living or dead, is coincidental and not intended by the author.

No part of this book may be reproduced, or stored in a retrieval system, or transmitted in any form or by any means, electronic, mechanical, photocopying, recording, or otherwise, without express written permission of the publisher.

ISBN-13: 979-8703562635

Cover design by: Art Painter
Library of Congress Control Number: 2018675309
Printed in the United States of America

CHAPTER 1

~~~~~ 🙙 ~~~~~

A small wooden cabin, secluded and hidden from the rest of the world, stood at the height of 6,000 ft. from the sea level, on a mountain among the Spruce Jungle ranges. This particular mountain was called "Mount Jett" by the local people. It was the highest peak among the mountains of the Spruce Jungle ranges, with its peak at the height of approximately 14,000 ft. from the sea level. Though the cabin was newly built, it looked crude with a rugged finish. It was located on the Northwest face of Mount Jett. The cabin was a temporary setup for a mission of a few weeks to months, depending on how fast the task would complete.

It was a moon-bleached, star-flecked, mid-summer night. The cabin was surrounded by spruce and pine trees, which stood like devils in the darkness. Jacob, a tall aesthetic man over 6 ft., tanned, handsome and cowboy kind of a guy, in his mid-thirties, wearing summer cotton clothes, a white T-shirt and brown shorts, emerged from the cabin, holding a bottle of beer in his left hand and a bowl of roasted peanuts in his right. He sat on a wooden chair sketchily shaped by himself, in front of the campfire that he'd lit a few minutes ago. It was a lovely comfortable evening with a warm breeze hitting against his body. A pint of chilled beer in his hand made the moment more relaxing and exciting.

His cabin had two rooms and a porch. A living room containing an old cosy couch with a pull out bed, a dining table, and at one corner was a small space for a kitchen. Leading ahead was a small bedroom, with a soft bed, a tiny refrigerator, a window that was more of a casement and an attached bathroom.

Jacob was in a pleasant, chipper mood and hummed a romantic tune. As he gulped a mouthful of chilled beer, he watched the several villages down at the foot of the mountain. The villages and towns looked like patches of lit colonies on the vast plain landscape, surrounded by the mountainous terrains. He also watched the other mountain peaks of the jungle ranges illuminated against the moonlit and star-spangled crystal clear sky. His gaze stopped at the summit of Mount Jett, and he sighed, assessing its tremendous height. He got out of the chair and placed some hay for his horse tied to the trunk of a nearby pine tree. He also put a bucket of water within the horse's reach.

While the horse was busy chewing the hay, Jacob stroked its back dearly and said, 'Hey there, my lucky Thunder, do you like the locale?' he asked the horse as if he were a human and his companion. Thunder, the horse, raised his neck and looked at Jacob with intense brown eyes, nodding his head and wagging his tail. He was a strikingly handsome black stallion with brown patches on his forehead, nose, and all four ankles.

Jacob, realizing that the bottle of beer in his hand was now empty, went inside to get another bottle from the refrigerator. As he opened the refrigerator door and gripped the second pint of beer with his right hand, he heard a sound of movement outside, from the direction of the bedroom window overlooking the backyard of the cabin. Jacob looked at the ajar window and was astonished to see a dark silhouette of a person standing outside the window, against the silvery grey of the sky. He was shocked and dashed towards the window with great curiosity to see who it was. But did not see anyone as the person outside the window had moved away from that site. Though Jacob opened the casement completely and peeped out, he saw no one.

Gracious! I thought I was alone here, all by myself. Who the hell is trying to stalk me? How could anyone dare to come near my cabin? He dashed out, hurried towards the back of the cabin and tried scanning the surrounding area and behind the tall trees with wide trunks. *There couldn't be anyone living at least a mile around my cabin. So I couldn't expect anyone here at my cabin, at this hour.* He was the kind of person who feared nothing. But this incident disturbed him a bit. He came back and sat on the chair in front of the campfire. The chair creaked as he sat on it, but he did not mind. His head was occupied with disturbing thoughts due to that incident and several incidents which had taken place since morning.

He had arrived on the mountain a month back and had started to construct the cabin. This day he had finished building it and was contented with his work. Though it was a crude construction, he decided that it was ideal for him, for his brief errand. He had visited a grocery and had bought food and other commodities that afternoon, from a village situated down at the mountain's foothill. He was glad he had almost settled and was delighted to commence the actual task, the next day.

What the hell! Unexpected and peculiar things had kept happening since morning. That morning at the crack of dawn, while he was getting ready to go for a jog, he had noticed that his jogging shoes were missing. *Who would want my boots? And why?* He had tried looking around for his shoes, thinking he could have misplaced them, but in vain. He had ignored the issue at that moment, deciding to look for them later. He couldn't have afforded to waste his precious time looking around and thus had dropped the idea of going for a jog, as he had a long day ahead.

When he had opened the refrigerator to pick the eggs for his breakfast at sunrise, he had noticed that the only two apples he had in store were missing. He recalled keeping the apples in the refrigerator just the previous evening, and now they were gone. He had ignored the missing apples as well.

That evening, when he had returned to the cabin with the commodities and other essentials, he had noticed that the white turkey towel that he'd hung and clipped for drying in the porch was gone as well and nowhere to be found. *This is crazy! If I keep losing my things like this, how am I gonna live here for the next couple of weeks? Who the hell is it, stealing my things? Whoever it is, is he a casual trespasser? Or a passing robber? Or someone in hideout like me, in the same locale as mine?* He had felt kind of odd and had smelt trouble around the corner. To top-up, he'd just then seen the silhouette of a person outside his window but had found no one in the vicinity when he'd tried to search. These incidents created an unwanted commotion within his head. He couldn't even decide whether the matter was of concern or whether he could ignore it. *If these things continue to happen, I will no longer tolerate this nuisance. I'll have to do something about it. I'll have to undertake some serious action,* he decided. Nothing queer happened for the rest of the night. He was tired and slept soundly through the night.

~ ~ ~ ~

Early the next morning at sunrise, Jacob made his way to the nearby lake to take a swim and freshen himself up for the day. When he neared the lake, he saw a person swimming in it, something like thirty yards away from its shore. *Gosh!* He hid behind a small boulderstone and watched, trying to figure out who the person in the lake was. From that distance, he couldn't distinctly discern whether the person in the lake was a boy or a girl, a man or a woman.

He advanced a little closer; he was astonished to see his jogging shoes and towel lying alongside each other on the grass, at the lake-shore. He looked at the person in the lake. He was happy that the thief was found effortlessly. On a closer look, he discerned that the person in the lake was a girl, swimming like a fish, something like thirty yards away from him. As the carefree girl stroked and crawled efficiently through the cold water, she happened to look at Jacob by chance. She panicked, immediately took a deep breath, dived into the water and disappeared underwater in a flash.

Good God! Who is she? What is she doing here all alone in the middle of nowhere? He looked around to inspect if anyone else was with her but saw no one. He waited for the girl to reappear in the vicinity for some time, but she didn't. He wondered how long she was going to stay underwater. *This is unbelievable! Is she a mermaid or some goddess of the jungle? If she is a human being, how could she be so fearless to live alone in this wilderness of the mountains? She has to be a human being; otherwise, she wouldn't have stolen my things. Is there any chance that she could make herself visible to me again? She looked pretty, though!* Her enticing, attractive face as he had fleetingly glimpsed at, just a moment ago, flashed like a wave in front of his eyes. An electricity of euphoria prickled his skin. He was enthralled and eager to see her again. He had to find her and make sure that she was indeed there.

He removed his T-shirt and got into the waters. He shuddered as the chill water in the lake covered his chest and back, seeping a kind of thrill into his gut. He swam to the approximate spot where he thought he had seen her and looked around with great hope and expectation to see her again. He felt genuinely disappointed when he could not see her anywhere around. He did not want to give up looking for her.

'Hey there, where are you?' he shouted for her. 'I've seen you. Please come out of the water. I won't hurt you.'

Forthwith, he heard some harsh sounds of the rippling water behind him and looked back. There the girl emerged on to the surface of the water, a little away from him, breathless for oxygen. She inhaled deeply to fill her lungs with enough oxygen and started to swim with a faster pace in the opposite direction.

'Hey you, wait there. I'm not a foe- stop, we can

be friends,' he shouted after her, as he chased, trying to close in on her.

When she heard his firm but caring voice, she turned back and looked at him with wide, fluttering, apprehensive dark eyes. She looked scared, but he gazed at her in awe, thinking she was one sweet, pretty little thing and her beautiful face left him flabbergasted. He guessed that she could be in her mid-twenties. She almost stopped swimming as she was tired, remained motionless and kept looking at him, shivering with cold and fear. He stopped swimming as well. He was captivated by her beauty and gazed into her sparkling blue eyes, as the water drops dripped from her dark hair onto her clean pink flawlessly flushed face. She was enthralled as well, as she kept looking at the attractive contour of Jacob's tanned face and squared-shoulders. For a moment, Jacob was curious to know what the angelic girl was doing in the middle of the jungle, on the remote mountain. He swam closer to her while she remained motionless like a statue without trying to escape. He gently stroked her cheek to confirm she was real. *Of course, she is real and as pretty as a picture.* He experienced a frisson of excitement.

As he slowly touched her cheeks, she blinked several times and said. 'Please forgive me for stealing your things and I'm sorry if I unintentionally caused you any inconvenience. I didn't mean to trouble you. I'm in a big mess myself,' saying so; she looked at him with a hope that he would forgive her. But he kept looking at her in surprise, without saying anything. 'Won't you forgive me?' she asked again.

He came out of his reverie and remarked, still looking at her alluring eyes. 'Certainly, I would. How could I not forgive such a lovely girl like you?' She looked glad.

The duo swam towards the edge of the lake, and Jacob helped her climb out of it. Olivia was wearing a white cotton shirt that stuck to her body, revealing the contour of her slim womanly figure, and yellow shorts from which the water dripped down on to her lean, long white legs. He took his stolen towel, which she had kept on the ground and slowly wiped her brownish dark, shoulder-length hair. He also gently wiped the water from her unblemished pink face with a few freckles on her cheeks and wrapped her shoulders with the towel.

'Come, let's go to my cabin,' Jacob invited. 'You can freshen and warm up there. Then we can talk,' he said as he held her hand and directed her towards his cabin. She looked glad and nodded her head. She walked alongside him, after wearing his jogging boots that were, in fact, too big for her feet.

After she freshened up, she came out of his bedroom, feeling warm and lively, wearing one of his T-shirts and a trouser. Jacob was waiting for her at the dining table with a breakfast of scrambled eggs and toast. The aroma of black coffee boiling on the stove filled her nostrils with excitement.

'Please join me for breakfast,' Jacob invited.

'The eggs and toast look delicious and inviting. It's almost two days since I have had a proper breakfast or a meal. Thank you so much,' she said, seating herself on the chair in front of him.

'I'm Jacob. Who are you? May I know your name?' He introduced himself to her, extended his right hand to shake hands with her.

She shook hands with him and said, 'I'm Olivia. You must be wondering what I am doing here. You must be thinking I'm crazy,' she said, putting a bite of scrambled egg into her mouth with a fork.

'Of course, I am curious.... go on...,' Jacob said, bringing the coffee kettle on to the dining table and pouring the black coffee into two mugs and offering one to her.

'I'm kind of lost right now,' she continued to talk, sipping her coffee. 'Hope you don't mind giving me shelter for a few days before I can pull myself together and get puffed on my way,' she looked at him hopefully.

'Certainly, you can stay with me as long as you

like, but first, you must have breakfast and tell me, what are you doing here and what trouble are you in?' he asked.

'I'm a girl from a village at the base of the mountain. There are several villages and towns out there at these mountains' foothill. My village is Figlington. You can as well see my village from here,' she said and continued, as she gobbled up her breakfast and sipped on her coffee.

'Back in Figlington, I was working as a waitress in a small hotel called Gill's inn, before I ended up here. The hotel owner Freddie is an old and kind man. His son has been my boyfriend for three years now. My boyfriend is kind of a hooligan and treats me like shit. He bosses over me all the time. He gets his jollies by harassing and embarrassing me in all possible ways. Initially, at the beginning of our friendship, he was very kind and cared a lot about me. I failed to understand that he acted like that to trap me in his selfish meaningless love. So I ignorantly started to live with him, against my parents' advice. But after experiencing all the ill-treatment bestowed upon me by my evil-crazy boyfriend, I got truly exhausted. I feel ashamed that I fell for this vandal and his charm, even after knowing about his bad conduct towards other people. I was getting nothing but a raw deal at his hands. I was helpless, and there was no choice but to escape.' Olivia looked relieved and comfortable at the moment and not like how she had seemed apprehensive, by the lake.

'I don't feel worthy enough even to show my star-crossed, ill-fated face to my parents. So I left a letter to my parents saying I was going away, would be fine and that they should never try to search for me. In the letter, I have assured them that I would write to them often. I am their only child. I escaped from my boyfriend and my village three days back and ended up on this mountain.

While I was hiding out and trying to figure out what to do next, I happened to see you and your cabin, here. I needed good shoes as my shoes were worn out. I needed a towel as well, as I'd forgotten to get one in a hurry.'

Olivia looked at Jacob with guilt and continued, 'I'm very sorry for having barged in into your territory without warning and for stealing your belongings. But I think I'm kind of lucky that you turned out to be a nice guy; otherwise, I would be finished,' she shivered.

Jacob was surprised to know that Olivia was on the run. 'Where did you stay during the last three days, and what did you eat?' he asked with concern.

'I had a backpack with me when I left the village with some food and things I needed. I have a camping tent fixed on the other side of the lake, but I do not feel safe at all. The food I'd brought with me lasted for two days. Yesterday I couldn't help stealing your apples. Last two nights, I couldn't even sleep well in this wilderness due to the fear of some wild animal attacking me and the apprehension of being found by my boyfriend. I guess I can call him my ex because I don't consider him my boyfriend anymore and I don't even want to utter his name. I hate him so much now,' Olivia said, looking restless.

The mountain range was vast, and Jacob's cabin was in a secret place too. He thought that it was just a coincidence that she happened to hide in the area, closer to his cabin and that it was destiny that he'd met her. He was sure that nobody would find her if she stayed with him for a few days.

'I'm so sorry for your plight. But no worries. You can stay with me in my cabin, and you don't have to be scared of me. I would do everything I can to safeguard you. Anyway, I'm staying here on this mountain temporarily for a couple of weeks on an assigned task. By the time I am done with my errand and want to leave this place, you would have figured what to do next with your life,' he assured.

'You mean... you'll let me stay here as long as you are here?' asked Olivia in an excited tone. She had developed an immediate liking for Jacob. He nodded his head in approval. 'My ex-boyfriend is a very rough and tough guy. He might come in search of me all over the mountains. He knows the mountains in and out. I mean that's what he thinks. I have written to my father in the letter that I'm going away to a far off city. So if my ex tries to find out from my father about my whereabouts, he might think I'm somewhere far away in a far off city. So, that is the only hope that he might not prowl for me in these mountains. But you never know. At the same time, I do not want to bring you any trouble by staying with you. So I think it will be better if I stayed for a day or two and quit from your place as early as possible,' she suggested.

'Never mind, you don't have to be scared of anything here. Just relax and take some rest before you decide what to do next,' he assured, while she looked at him with gratitude.

'Jacob, I'm surprised and curious about you as well. You look like an outsider to these regions. What are you doing here? It feels like God has sent you to protect me,' said Olivia.

He smiled at her remark and said, 'I am kind of an adventure fanatic. I think it's just destiny and a coincidence that I happened to be here when you needed help.' They were done with their breakfast and came out of the cabin onto the porch.

'Is that your horse?' Olivia asked, looking admiringly at his stunningly gorgeous stallion.

'Yes, he's my horse. His name is Thunder. He has been my companion past ten years, and we've developed a great bonding midst us. We understand each other very well, and Thunder has won a couple of races for me too.' Jacob said proudly, directing her towards the horse.

'Hey there Thunder, say hi to Olivia,' he introduced Olivia to Thunder. Thunder sniffed and nodded his head.

'Wow! He understood what you said to him,' said Olivia, laughing with amusement. She patted and stroked Thunder with love and kissed the stallion on his face. The horse sniffed again as if he were trying to make friends with her. Jacob and Olivia strolled in front of the cabin and came to the mountain's edge with a steep terrain ahead. She showed him her village, pointing at a few clusters of houses and roads neath the mountain's north face. As they returned to the cabin, she asked with interest. 'Jacob, are you married?'

'Nope,' he said instantly. 'If I were married, I wouldn't be here all by myself. I once had a girlfriend, and her name was Sophia. She died of blood cancer six years back. After her death, I was very much lost. To cope with the sorrow, I dedicated myself to my work, which is, of course, my passion,' he said with a gloomy expression.

'I'm sorry for your loss, Jacob,' she said, looking at him in shock. She thought for a while and said hopefully. 'I have a request, Jacob. Please promise me that you will never tell anyone down in the villages about me if at all you happened to be there any time.'

'Don't you worry, Olivia. You're going to be my little secret, and I promise you that no one will ever come to know about your hideout, from my side. But I have one condition,' he said firmly. She looked at him nervously as he continued. 'If you want to stay here with me in my cabin, you must never be curious about my pattern of work and my errand. It would be best if you never asked me anything about my job here, and never snoop around to find out anything about my job. That is a rule. If you agree to it, I can let you stay with me as long as you want,' he said with a firm but polite voice.

Olivia's priority was to obtain a temporary shelter for herself before she could think her situation through. So she immediately agreed to his rule, as it did not seem like a big deal at the moment. She looked at his steely but sincere brown eyes and decided to trust him.

'Is there any possibility you would get visitors any time to this abode of yours on business?' She asked in doubt.

'As far as possible...no. If at all yes, not daily, though, - maybe a couple of times that's all. But you will be given prior intimation, and you can hide without anybody knowing about your presence around here,' he said with confidence. She thanked him heartily.

Before he went away on his errand, he suggested that she could rest on his bed in the bedroom. She bid him goodbye for the day, and as soon as she laid herself on his fluffy bed, she fell fast asleep - all her worries and challenges melted in her sweet dreams as she slept like a baby.

CHAPTER 2

~~~~~ ☐ ~~~~~

That evening, Jacob returned to his cabin before sunset and Olivia was still slumbering on his bed. For a moment, he stood at the door of the bedroom and looked at her perfect, pretty face. She appeared calm and peaceful, sleeping like an angel. He did not want to disturb her beatific sleep. So he just stood by the door, watching her. He couldn't take his eyes off her as he watched her long eyelashes resting peacefully on her high freckled cheeks. *She is one perfect little being I've ever seen,* he thought. As he feasted his eyes on her for a while, she slowly opened her eyes and sat up, on the bed, completely disoriented of the time and place. She looked at him in shock and blinked several times. He behaved as if he'd arrived just then.

'I'm sorry, Jacob. I think I slept too long. What time is it, and when did you return?' She asked in surprise, fluttering her eyelids several times. 'You must be tired after your day out. I'll make some coffee.' Saying so, she descended and hurriedly tried to go out of the bedroom towards the kitchen, past him.

In the process, she tripped at his feet and was about to fall headlong, when he clasped her slim waist at once and supported her with his brawny arms, protecting her from tumbling down. She held on to his arms tightly to get her balance when their eyes met.

She recovered instantly and said, 'Good God! How heedless of me! Thank you, Jacob. You are my saviour.' Saying so, she kissed him on his left cheek as an acknowledgement for his timely help.

'Take your time, Olivia. I'm in no hurry for a cup of coffee,' said Jacob, his gaze still fixed on her blue eyes. 'I'm glad you rested well today.'

'Yeah, sure I got my beauty sleep. Thank you for offering me your snugly bed to rest in,' she mumbled, still looking at him, while the two of them reluctantly got released from each other's embrace.

She looked at him with gratitude because he was very kind to her, which was a gladdening experience for her. She had not experienced this good feeling of being cared, in a long time. They sat in the porch and drank their coffee, munching crackers and watching the sunset.

'Look, Jacob! The sun is trying to hide behind the mountain ranges!' Olivia pointed at the peaks of the other mountains, at their panoramic view, where the orange ball of the cloud-streaked languorous sun slowly glided down behind the mountains. 'Wow, it's such a beautiful and celestial sight. I haven't enjoyed a sunset in a long, long time. I was always engrossed in my stupid job- trying to impress my boyfriend all the time, even though he was rude to me. I don't get it; what I saw in him, made me fall for his fake love. I spent my past few years in hell. Thank God, I somehow managed to escape from him. But I'm still apprehensive that he would be distraught and might come after me sooner,' she said anxiously with fear in her eyes.

'Don't you worry, Olivia,' said Jacob. 'Why are you thinking about your sad past while watching a beautiful sunset? Your past is nothing but water under the bridge now. You need to move on and enjoy your stay here. Don't think of anything that makes you feel unhappy. I would do everything I can to protect you while you are here with me. Promise me that you won't talk about your ex anymore or any other sad thing for that matter,' he advised her.

'I'm sorry, Jacob. I just got carried away. I promise I'll do as you say,' she said, resting her head on Jacob's squared-shoulder. The two of them watched the sun go down, glorying in the enchanting magic of all the jubilant colours of the skies. After sundown, the whole atmosphere became dark, cold and dull with a cool breeze brushing their enlivened skins. They sat silently for a while- listening to the birds' chirping and singing, watching them fly in flocks in search of places to roost.

Jacob and Olivia were kind of captivated in the comfort of each other and sat there for a long time in each other's company, saying nothing. It was a strange feeling- still so dear and cosy. The duo was smitten by each other. Jacob glided his hand towards her smooth, slender, white hand and caressed it with love, while she lifted her head and searched for the words in his eyes. His soft eyes met hers, and in a flash, their lips met as well. Even before they knew what was happening, they kissed each other a long passionate kiss. It felt so right and so complete. Jacob bent over her and pulled her closer, gripping the small of her back and neck with his firm, eager arms. They kissed again, and this time it was more sensual. He remembered his late girlfriend Sophia and backed off for a moment feeling at sea and looked at Olivia's face. Her eyes were closed, and she looked utterly lost like she was in the middle of a sweet dream. He delicately stroked aside her hair locks that floated on her face, with his fingers, watching her blushed face, as she slowly opened her eyes and looked at him questioningly.

'Olivia, I can't believe that we kissed. I'm sorry if I offended you. We are strangers,' he confessed.

Olivia came back to her senses and stuttered, 'True, Jacob. We need to know each other first. But I think I already like you a lot and I'm not offended,' she soothed, gazing at him with her heavy eyes.

'Thank you. Come on then, let's see what we have for dinner,' he said, smiling and winked at her as he stood up from his chair. Olivia smiled too, and the two of them went inside the cabin.

They had a hearty dinner of fish spaghetti and green salad. Later, Jacob made himself comfortable out in the living room, on the pull out bed from the couch, while Olivia slept for the night on his bed in the bedroom.

~ ~ ~ ~

That night, Olivia was woken up suddenly after midnight, by some distant thudding and hammering sounds. In the nights during the last four days of her stay on the mountains, she had heard the sounds two times before as well but had ignored them as they were faint. But today, she heard them a bit louder. She couldn't decide from which direction the sounds were coming. She tried to concentrate. The sounds were rhythmic as if someone was hammering on stones and mud like somebody was digging somewhere in the mountains. She was all ears and tried to locate their direction, but the sounds stopped. She tried to go back to sleep, but the sounds started to bang again after a gap of fifteen to twenty minutes.

Olivia lost her cool as her sleep got disturbed. She felt freaked out and curious at the same time. *Whatever is happening out here? Why do I hear these sounds only in the nights?* She got suspicious. She leapt out of bed and peered out of the window to see if she could find anything unusual. But found nothing. Anyway, she knew that the sounds did not come from the backyard.

Olivia slowly opened the bedroom door and peeped into the living room. It was dark there except for the dim moonlight that spilt inside through the slits of the partially open window. She looked at the couch and saw Jacob, fast asleep. As the night was cold, she noticed that he had wholly covered himself with a blanket and was sleeping tight. She did not want to disturb him. So, she tried to locate the direction of the thudding and hammering sounds again, but in vain. It felt like the sounds were coming from within herself.

For a moment, Olivia doubted if they were her hallucinations, as she was facing a tough and challenging time of her life at the moment. Her mind was haunted with rippling thoughts as she was scared that her horrible ex-boyfriend would come hunting for her, anytime.

She opened the main door of the cabin and came onto the porch. The dark vicinity with the ghostlike trees freaked her out even more. *Gosh! It's brutally cold and scary*; she immediately went back inside the cabin and back to bed. While she tried sleeping, she got used to the sounds after some time.

How come Jacob is fast asleep, even with these hammering sounds banging? Maybe he is genuinely spent after a long tiring day, out on the mountains. God must know where Jacob had been all day long. I'm not even allowed to ask him about what he does and where he goes. I guess I'm allowed to ask about the creepy sounds because they disturb my sleep and maybe they have nothing to do with his work. Henceforth, I'm not going to sleep during the day. Only then can I sleep well in the nights.

I don't have to worry about anything here because Jacob has promised to safeguard me and my only concern should be to stay here peacefully before I decide what to do next with my life. I don't have to bother about anything else. If the sounds were some trouble, Jacob certainly would have been concerned about them too. When he is least bothered and sleeping sound, why should I be bothered? What if Jacob hasn't heard the thudding sounds at all? What if he is in danger as well? Tomorrow night, If I hear those sounds again, I'm gonna alert him. If I do not hear them again, I will not mention it to him and just let it go. After some time before dawn, the sounds stopped, and Olivia fell asleep.

~ ~ ~ ~

Next morning, while Jacob and Olivia sat by the dining table having breakfast, Olivia felt impulsive to ask Jacob about the freaky sounds that she had heard the previous night.

'Jacob, yesterday night I heard some weird

thudding and hammering sounds all night, and I couldn't make out from which direction the sounds were coming. I tried my best to concentrate and find the source of the sounds and their direction but in vain. Did you hear them as well?'

Jacob seemed undisturbed from what she said, instead, kept looking at her pretty face and her innocent expressions, as he ate his breakfast. 'Nope', that was all he said.

She felt a little guilty for asking him questions. She got confused. *I'm not allowed to ask only about him and his work. I guess it's OK if I ask him about the weird sounds.* 'Did you hear the sounds as well, Jacob?' she repeated the question with confidence.

'I was fast asleep. So I did not hear any unusual sounds in the night,' he answered. 'Moreover, I've already assured you that you are going to be safe here. You need not worry about any unusual sounds or anything for that matter. I'm here to take care of everything. So do not bother yourself again, if you hear any sounds. Such sounds are commonly heard in the mountains. It's not a big issue because we will not get hurt. These are huge mountain ranges. Weird sounds keep coming from different directions; you never know why and from where. You'll have to let the matter go,' he said with a firm but a calm voice.

Olivia felt scared that if she bothered him with

such questions still further, he might throw her out of his cosy, safe cabin. She decided to ignore the matter about the sounds and kept silent. After breakfast, Jacob left as usual, astride on his horse, promising to return before sundown.

After she saw him out, Olivia spent her day tidying the cabin and arranging Jacob's belongings in the best possible way she could. She went to her tent on the other side of the lake and brought all her belongings to Jacob's cabin. She had a few of her clothes, a photo of her parents and a few of her favourite décor things in her backpack, which she unpacked and organized neatly. She changed the couch's position and direction, and the dining table, making the living room look more spacious. She scoured a few burnt utensils and mopped the floor. She made a few curtains for the windows with a shawl she had. As Jacob had promised that he would return to the cabin by eventide, she made dinner for the two of them.

As expected, he arrived before sunset and was very glad that the dinner was ready, the dining table set and the interior of the cabin was in apple-pie order.

Jacob lit the campfire in front of the cabin. The duo sat on the wooden chairs by the campfire, alongside each other and sipped on the wine he'd got from town. They remained silent for some time. Olivia did not know whether she could ask him about his day. He took a swig of the wine, looking intently and admiringly at her.

'Looks like you have had your hands full at the cabin today. You've done a great job with all the cleaning, cooking and some creative work with the interiors as well,' Jacob appreciated, scrutinizing the curtains. 'I'm glad that you're trying to make yourself comfortable here with me. If you need anything from the town during your stay here, you are free to ask me. I would gladly bring them for you,' he said, taking another gulp of the astringent wine.

She looked lovingly at him, feeling a little tipsy. 'Right now, I do not need anything else, Jacob. I am just comfortable and can improvise with whatever is available here. I feel so happy and safe being with you, and that is what matters to me,' she said fondly, stroking his nose with her index finger.

'If you feel bored during the day, you can go for a swim in the lake but be careful that no one finds you like I did the other day,' he said with a mischievous sparkle in his eyes. 'If you need any books to read, I can get them for you. There's a big central library downtown,' he pointed at the vast cluster of lights spread-out at the foothill of the mountain.

'Yes, I know that town,' she said, looking towards where he pointed, 'It's the town of Wimberley. It's something like 25 miles away from my village. I've been to the town many times. I've also been to the central library there, I guess, a few times with my father,' she said remembering the times she'd spent with her father as a young girl and looked a little gloomy and sad.

'OK, anyway, I already have a few books with me on history, philosophy and travel. You can read them for now if you want to,' Jacob said. Olivia was overwhelmed by the amount of care Jacob was lavishing upon her. Her ex-boyfriend had never spoken to her with such concern. She remembered the times when her ex-boyfriend kicked and ridiculed her. *He was so brutal*; tears appeared in her sparkling blue eyes. She looked at Jacob, and he was worried that he had somehow offended her. She didn't know how to react to his humane concern towards her. Jacob smiled at her when Olivia pecked his cheeks with love.

Olivia got up from her chair; sat on the ground beside Jacob's legs; placed her head on his laps and sat looking dreamily towards the fire. He smoothly ran his fingers through her silky loose hair. When the bottle of wine was empty, they decided to have dinner in the porch itself. The two of them went in and brought the plates. She had prepared macaroni, strawberry yoghurt and some salad. The two of them had a hearty dinner and went to bed. Jacob slept on the couch in the living room while Olivia slept on his bed in the bedroom, like the previous night.

~ ~ ~ ~

That night, in the wee small hours, she was woken up again by the thudding and hammering sounds. She was petrified this time. She made her supreme efforts to ignore the sounds because Jacob had advised her to do so. *If these weird sounds are coming from somewhere else, why should they seem like they are coming from within the cabin or my head? Why are they heard only in the bewitching hours of the night and not during the day? These sounds are bothersome. I've got to find the source of these thudding and hammering sounds.*

She hurried out to the living room and found that Jacob was sleeping on his couch as tight as ever. She did not want to alarm and vex him. *Poor Jacob, he must be exhausted. He is not even aware of the thudding sounds at the moment. I must explore and discover the source of the sounds myself.*

Olivia wrapped herself in a blanket to protect herself from the frosty cold weather on the mountain, went out of the cabin and looked around to do a reconnaissance. The sounds had halted for a while. She sat in the patio, waiting for the sounds to reappear again.

The sounds started to bang again after a few minutes and seemed they were looming from behind the cabin. Olivia dashed towards the backyard and tried to listen carefully. She piled up all her courage and searched behind the rocks and around the trees. Now, the sounds seemed like they were coming from the front yard. She dashed to the cabin's front.

There was about an acre of an ample open space of grassy land in front of the porch, slightly bumpy, bare, rocky and sloping, with very few trees here and there. It was steep at the edge of the open space, with a view of a small village down there. She went to the edge of the cliff and stared at the moonlit, light-specked village. Very few dim golden yellow lights flickered down from the village. For a moment, it seemed like the sounds were coming from the village below. The wind was blowing briskly and kept changing its directions. So she was confused about the direction of the sounds again. Sometimes the sounds were louder and other times dull. She gave up her attempt and decided to ignore the sounds, even if she heard them every day.

When Jacob is so cool about these sounds and sleeping soundly, why can't I do the same? Soon the sounds stopped. She strolled a little while in front of the cabin, trying to figure out what was happening, and then she went back into the cabin.

When she entered the living room from outside, she was shocked to see that Jacob was wide awake and sitting on the couch with his blanket on his laps. He seemed like he had just woken up and wondering what the sounds were.

'Where had you been, Olivia?' he asked flummoxed, seeing her entering the living room from outside. Olivia felt guilty because she knew he would disapprove of her sneaking around the cabin, especially in the witching hours of the night.

'Jacob, I heard the creepy thudding and hammering sounds again tonight. I couldn't sleep, as I was frantic with concern. I didn't mean to alarm you,' she admitted, trying to conceal her angst. 'Why are you awake? Did you hear them as well?' She asked him curiously.

'Yes, I heard them too. If you were worried, you should have woken me up. Why are you endangering yourself by going out alone in the dead of night? What if you get hurt?' he asked, all solicitous.

'Are you going to send me away, Jacob? Are you mad at me?' Olivia asked innocently.

'Come on, don't be a child. Why should I send you away? I'm not gonna do anything of that sort because you haven't asked anything about my work,' he mollified. 'Yes, I heard the sounds too. I've been hearing them for some nights during the past month of my stay here. Like you, I initially freaked out as well, but later on, I got accustomed to the sounds, and now I don't hear them anymore, even though they exist. You better do the same thing; ignore. Come here and sit near me,' he waved her towards the couch. She was glad that he was not angry with her for being a sneaky bugbear, so she went and sat beside him. He hugged her, and she felt warm and folksy.

'Jacob, can I sleep on the couch with you today? I feel anxious about the whole thing. I cannot understand what is happening to me and my life. Everything is so new, so strange and so uncertain. I am completely puzzled over,' Olivia admitted, thinking deeply. He kissed her on her forehead and agreed to her request. The two of them slept on the couch, holding each other. She felt safe and secure and cherished the moment. All her anxiety vanished in no time, and she fell deep asleep, in his warm embrace.

CHAPTER 3
~~~~~ ⬚ ~~~~~

Olivia slept carefree in Jacob's protective arms till the sun rays hit her eyes in the morning through the open window. When she opened her eyes, she saw Jacob getting ready for his day out.

'Good morning, hey,' he winked at her and smiled.

'Morning, Jacob. You should have woken me up early. I could have prepared breakfast for you.' Olivia said, stretching her body on the bed, in a state of languor.

Breakfast and coffee were waiting for her on the dining table. As she joined Jacob at the breakfast table after a few minutes, Olivia so very much wanted to ask him about his schedule for the day and why he was going out so early. *Mind your own business Olivia*; she cautioned herself.

'Olivia, today I am receiving two visitors this morning at the cabin. Two men who are my work partners. So you better be inside the bedroom when they are around and never come out till they are gone. They might arrive here anytime now,' he cautioned her.

'OK, Jacob. Thanks a lot for forewarning me,' she said.

Soon after having breakfast, Olivia went inside

the bedroom and closed the bedroom door behind her. She also decided to close the bedroom window, though it had a curtain. When she made her way towards the bedroom window, she saw two horsemen trotting on the rough lane towards the cabin from among the trees behind the cabin.

She was a little nervous. *Good God! How I wished no one would ever come near this cabin anytime. It looks like this cabin is not entirely secluded. Am I in danger?* She was ill at ease. She immediately moved aside to conceal herself from being seen and sat on the bed, trying to regain her composure. *What work does Jacob have with these two men? What kind of a job do they have on this remote mountain? Am I safe here?* She was too nervous again and failed to calm herself down. She kind of felt annoyed that Jacob had invited some strangers into his abode, where she was hiding like a refugee.

Olivia, you must be grateful to Jacob because he has offered you shelter and promised to protect you. You must be thankful that he even informed you about the strange men's arrival beforehand; she tried justifying and soothing herself to get the grip of the situation. She heard the sounds of the galloping horses outside the window and sat still, biting her nails, doubting whether she was really in safe hands.

The two horsemen dismounted from their horses in the front yard. Jacob walked towards them and exchanged greetings with them.

'Hello, Jacob. I am Peter, and this is Brayan. Nice to meet you. It looks like you're almost settled in, and ready for the job,' said one of the guys.

'Hello there Peter, and hello Brayan,' Jacob welcomed the two men. 'Of course, I'm all set and ready for the show. Good to meet you too. I was told about your arrival a week back and glad to see the two of you here on time, as expected. So, when did you guys arrive at this destination and how was your journey?' he asked, offering them coffee, as they sat on chairs in the porch talking about each other's welfare.

Peter, a man in his early forties, slurped his coffee and said, 'I arrived a week back, and I'm staying in a motel, in the town of Wimberley, down the mountain. During the last week, I did some preliminary work regarding our mission,' he said.

'What about you, Brayan?' Jacob asked, looking at Brayan, a young man in his late twenties.

'I arrived a week back too and fixed a tent for myself on the south face of Mount Jett,' said Brayan. 'Wolfe, the middleman, gave me details about Peter and his stay at Wimberley. Wolfe had instructed me to meet Peter today. So I met him by the White River, and he brought me here to meet you.'

'OK, that's great. let me tell you about myself,' said Jacob. 'I was instructed by Wolfe to get here and settle down on Mount Jett, to do my part of the homework, before the two of you arrived. So I arrived here a month back and built this cabin to stay in. I have tried to study and know the mountain, and it's terrain a bit, though not completely. I am advised that, though the three of us are strangers to each other, we need to work with complete harmony and trust,' he said.

He stopped for a moment as if he remembered something and continued, 'Do you have any idea about the kingpin, the taskmaster, who hired us?' he asked.

'We have been in communication only with the middleman, who calls himself "Wolfe",' said Peter. 'But I'm well aware that there is one person, a mastermind behind the whole mission and his nickname is "THE ROARK". Brayan, do you know Roark's actual name?' asked Peter.

'Of course not. I know Roark by his nickname only. Like you both, Wolfe, the middleman hired me, instructing me to work for Roark,' replied Brayan. 'Do you know anything else about Roark?' asked Brayan to Peter.

'Certainly, I know a little about the kingpin. Needless to say, Roark, who is the mastermind behind our mission, whatever his real name is, is staying on a private island among the Atlantics. He is supposedly very caring towards his employees, especially the sincere ones. Roark remunerates and rewards his employees handsomely for the bonafide and honest services they give, to make his missions successful. But he is a perisher of the dishonest ones.

So I want us to work candidly towards this mission so that Roark is happy with us and would reward us handsomely,' said Peter. 'In the last two of his missions, I have worked for him and have done a good job. In both the missions, I happened to work with different teams containing strangers all together and was rewarded quite handsomely for my truthful and loyal contributions.'

'This is my first participation in Roark's missions,' said Jacob. 'Do you think we can do this job ourselves, without being under Roark's mercy? We can keep all the profits to ourselves and share among the three of us. What do you guys say to this idea? Anyway, there is no one around here to supervise and keep an eye on us, right?' asked Jacob.

Brayan was happy to hear this because he was young, a foolhardy and very enthusiastic to make a fortune faster through shortcut routes. 'I think it's a brilliant idea. This project is my second one with Roark. The first time, I worked truthfully. But I was partly successful, and Roark did not pay me enough. Maybe he was not happy with the quality of my work. It was an utter waste of my time and energy, but I could decipher a lot from my first job with him,' he said.

Brayan continued turning to Jacob, 'Anyway, Peter and myself have already worked in Roark's missions before, and we've got the hang of it. Moreover, Wolfe told me that you are an archaeologist and skilled in performing this kind of job, though it's your first mission with Roark. Undoubtedly, the three of us could make a good team to make this mission a success. We could share the major part of the profits among ourselves,' he said, trying to discuss more on the plot.

But Peter was against that idea. 'It's a bad idea. Let's not go astray. We are hired to do this job for Roark, who is highly influential and invincible. If we are under the mercy of this guy, we will remain safe.

As you know, it's a big network of underworld business. We are just a small straw of hay among the lot. We are petty employees. They have given us all the details and instructions to go about the job. It would be foolishness to even think of cheating Roark. It is always better to be under the mercy of someone influential like him. He is the person who hired us and is supposedly loyal, a man of his words. He takes care of his employees very well. This way, we don't have to worry about our safety. We just do our job honestly and get a handsome reward.

Moreover, all three of us are strangers, and we do not know if anyone of us is Roark's spy. If at all we tried to cheat Roark, we are finished. We all must bear that in mind. So let's not rock the boat,' cautioned Peter.

Jacob agreed to what Peter said. 'Yes, you are right, Peter. It's better, to be honest, and loyal. Why risk our lives unnecessarily by going adrift? This mission is my first project with Roark, and I better be diligent and careful not to betray the kingpin. I was just curious to know what would happen to us if we tried cheating on him. I feel curious about this employer of ours. Has any one of you seen him anytime? How I wish I could get a chance to meet him sometime!' said Jacob.

'Of course, not. Roark is a myth,' said Peter. Nobody in the network has seen him. Also, no one knows who works for him. He has been in this underworld business for many years and is well versed in trading illegal goods. He has connections all over the world with trade icons. He has several middlemen working for him. Even the middlemen haven't seen him in person if I'm right.

Roark hires different people for different projects, mediated by his middlemen. The middlemen also never show themselves to any employees. Every time a group of strangers are hired and brought together. Despite being strangers to each other, the employees need to work in harmony to succeed in the project. Everything is meticulously organized and well-run. All communications happen secretly on phone calls only. Moreover, I'm aware that few of his hardcore spies, supervising the teams in secret, see to it that none of the employees would even think of betraying Roark. Maybe one among us might be a spy as well, you never know,' he said, and all the three of them looked at each other's faces in suspicion.

Peter continued, 'If by chance any member in the team tries to cheat, I wager, the betrayer is punished; in fact, he will be killed and buried. No one will ever come to know what happened to him,' he said.

Listening to Peter, Brayan looked a little panicked for even thinking of cheating. 'I know, the whole thing is meticulously carried out with high fidelity. It's better to endeavour truthfully towards our assigned job,' he finally agreed too. The three employees of the current mission, looked at each other again leerily, trying to study if anyone among them was Roark's spy.

Jacob looked concerned. 'I'm an archaeologist myself and have been working for the federal-state all these years. Two months back, I received a phone call from this middleman, Wolfe, who asked me if I was interested in working for Roark. At first, I shilly-shallied to go against the law, but Wolfe told me that my safety was their foremost responsibility. I said yes because the offer made to me was quite fetching and I was itching for some real adventure in my life too, bored with my routine barren work. I accepted the offer because I thought it was worth the try, as he assured me of complete safety with great fortune and escapade,' he said. 'By the way, Peter, how was your experience working for Roark in your previous projects?'

'Of course, it has been great,' said Peter. 'This is my third project, and I'm happy with the offers made to me as well, with complete safety. Roark has always paid me attractively, as promised. He has never ones budged from his promises. Still, working for Roark is like playing with fire. The unknown Godfather is as dangerous as he is truthful. Loyalty is his mantra, and he cannot bear cheaters,' he stressed the point again.

'OK, all three of us are strangers. We have met here with one plan, being hired by one employer. So let's go ahead with our mission with a high-five,' concluded Jacob and all three of them high-fived each other.

'OK, what was your progress in the last two days, Jacob?' Peter asked.

'I was on the east face in the last two days,' said Jacob. 'Of course, I couldn't make much progress. The whole thing is very complicated and complex. It's not that easy, especially for people like us who have set foot on this mountain for the first time. Though we are all good at our work, we need help from someone who knows these mountains well,' he said.

'Of course, you are right. I tried to cover the south face of Mount Jett during the last one week but to less avail,' said Brayan. 'We have to find someone familiar with these mountains who can guide us into finding the landmarks that we are after. Yesterday, I met a man in one of the villages down there. After talking to him casually, I reckoned that he knows the mountains quite well and he offered to help me,' he said.

'That's good, but did you tell him about our actual mission?' asked Jacob.

'Of course, not,' said Brayan. 'I simply told him that I was doing some research on the fossils and that I needed help. I did not tell him about the actual mission. He said he would help me if I paid him. I said I would talk through with my associates and let him know,' he said.

'OK, good job. Come on now, it's time we get going,' said Jacob.

Olivia could hear and perceive a few of their talks from inside the bedroom, though they were not clearly audible. She felt guilty for eavesdropping. *How could I be so poking? Why couldn't I just follow Jacob's rule and save myself from the outside world?*

The overall picture Olivia got to ascertain about their mission, from their scuttlebutt was - there existed a hardcore mastermind, a Kingpin known as "THE ROARK", who was highly influential and lived on a faraway private island. Jacob, Peter and Brayan were a temporary team of his employees to carry out some hush-hush mission on Mount Jett. It was going to be an underworld affair with a vast network. So was illegal and against the law. The employees would be well taken care of by Roark, as long as they remained truthful to the mission and would be rewarded handsomely and kept protected. At the moment, the three employees of the current mission were strangers to each other and were also spied upon by Roark's men.

Olivia was avidly curious to know about their secret mission, as she did not hear them mentioning anything about the actual project. *How pathetic of me! I'm not even allowed to ask Jacob anything about his work affairs. He is a kind man who has agreed to give me shelter, showing great care and love. I cannot afford to lose his trust by disobeying him. Moreover, I have nowhere else to go. I better keep my nose out of his business,* she decided.

CHAPTER 4

~~~~~ ◊ ~~~~~

Olivia heard footsteps approaching and became alert. In a flash, she took hold of a book and rested on the bed. She acted as if she was busy reading all the while. She did not want Jacob to suspect that she was overhearing their conversation and did not want to offend or upset him in any way.

Jacob came inside, closed the door behind him and whispered. 'You are an impeccable girl, a lily-white,' he said, bending over and kissing her on her forehead. 'I don't understand how anyone could be rude to you!'

Olivia smiled, looking at him dearly. Jacob then said he was leaving on a task, with the two men waiting outside.

'Olivia, you need to be heedful out here,' he cautioned her before leaving. 'Please do not come out of the cabin as far as possible, though I can ensure you that no one would be around here and that you would be safe. I want you to help me help you. I'll return before sunset.' Saying so, he held her face in his two hands and nuzzled at her nose. She felt so much loved and glanced at him speechless. He bid her goodbye for the day and left with the two horsemen on his errand.

After the three men galloped and raced away

from the cabin on their respective horses, Olivia who watched them from the window, prayed God to keep Jacob safe and make his task, whatever it was, worthwhile.

She now had to plan her errands for the day to spend her time fruitfully in the cabin. She took a refreshing shower and rested for a while on the couch, trying not to think anything negative. She remembered the events of the previous night. She smiled to herself, recalling the cosy warmth of Jacob's embrace, as they had slept together in each other's comfort on the pull out bed of the couch. *How I wish Jacob let me rest by his side, holding him, every day! He is an intense kind-hearted person. I am so lucky to have met him.*

For instance, she felt disturbed, thinking he had indulged in some illegal affair. *Whatever he is up to, I shouldn't be worrying about it. I know that I have started to fall in love with him, and I must have faith in him. I need his company and support, and that is all should matter to me at the moment. I must do everything I can, to keep him happy.*

Though she tried to trample down her disturbing thoughts, she felt restless again, thinking about the fact that he was undoubtedly into something felonious. She became apprehensive upon imagining Jacob being caught by the police and punished by law. *Don't you worry, Olivia. Nothing of that sort will happen;* she soothed herself and tried to put her pessimistic thoughts at bay and tried to contemplate all the cosy things that he was capable of offering her.

She tried to remember his face, as she had seen him the first time in the dark waters of the lake. *Damn! He is so handsome and has kind brown eyes.* She remembered the long kiss they had shared while watching the sunset and blushed by its mere thought. She realized that, that particular soul kiss with Jacob was the best she had ever experienced and felt pleased for having gotten an opportunity to stay with such a nonpareil man. She thanked her ex-boyfriend in her mind for having ill-treated her. Otherwise, she wouldn't have escaped from him and wouldn't have gotten a chance to meet Jacob.

After a bit of day-dreaming, Olivia decided to read one of Jacob's books. His collection of books were mostly on history, philosophy and travel. She randomly picked one book, went and sat on the couch, and looked at it. It happened to be a book on history and geography. Even before she could open the book, a folded piece of paper fell from it, onto her lap. Curiously she picked it up and unfolded it. It looked like some map. The map seemed very old, and on closer observation, she guessed it could be a map of the mountain ranges on which they were staying at the moment because she also found the name of the town Wimberley on the map. There were few marks made in red and green on the map, but she couldn't make heads or tails of those markings.

I better not interfere with Jacob's affairs; thinking so, she folded the map and placed it back between the book's pages. She also put back the book from where she'd picked it. She now looked around, trying to figure out how to spend her time. Though Jacob had cautioned her to be careful, she came out of the cabin to get some fresh air. Though it was summertime, it was cool and comfortable on the mountain at the height, around the cabin. She looked in all directions to make sure there was no soul around. When she thought it was quite safe, she decided to ramble among the trees, around the cabin.

She started to think about Jacob again. *I must never do anything to annoy Jacob, whatever the matter may be. I cannot afford to lose him because I love him truly, and I feel he loves me too. Jacob is the one who could make me feel complete. He is the one who is going to protect me. I have never met anyone like him before.*

She started to stroll behind the cabin, enjoying the zephyr among the pines and the hushful music of the singing birds. It was serene all around, and she rejoiced the sound of the whistling draught and the faint burble of the White River, flowing through the valleys.

She looked up at the canopy, created by leaves

of pine and spruce trees and enjoyed the view. Unexpectedly, she tripped upon something heavy and hard at her feet among the shrubs. She looked down and was surprised to see quite a big green bag safely placed among the shrubs as if it were hidden there. The bag's colour blended with that of the leaves and twigs of the shrubs and wasn't easily detectable if one wasn't watchful.

Whose bag is it? Why would anybody hide it here in the backyard? What is inside the bag? Is anybody plotting to hurt Jacob? Is he in danger? Am I in trouble? A thousand questions arose in her mind, and she grew fidgety. The more she tried to avoid her curiosity, the nearer she was being dragged to it. She was eager to find out what was in the bag. She looked around sceptically and saw no one. *What if this bag belonged to Jacob? Even if he is hiding something in the bag, it is none of my business to sneak a peek into it. It would be like betraying him if I peered at its contents without his permission. Suppose, it doesn't belong to him and there is something in the bag that is a menace to his life, and my life, I need to look at its contents to rule out any danger.*

She was perplexed and felt restless with turmoil in her head, whether to see the contents of the bag or not. It was easy to unzip the bag and peek into it. She again tried to caution herself. *Why should I even want to know what is there in the bag? Olivia, control yourself, it's none of your business*, she tried to ignore the bag but in vain. She vacillated for a few minutes, not able to decide whether to look into the bag or let it go.

She was too curious. She impulsively squatted on the ground and slowly unzipped the green bag. She saw some hardware tools in it. One looked like a kind of machine, something like a metal detector. Then there were other tools, a shovel, a dagger, a scoop, a trowel, a rock pick, a pry bar and many other devices which she couldn't even name them. Though she didn't know what they were exactly used for, they looked like the tools for digging and detecting- to be precise, the devices for a treasure hunt.

Some of the tools seemed like they were used recently. *Of course, Jacob is an archaeologist, and maybe these are his tools. Why is he hiding them here? He could have kept them in the cabin. Perhaps these tools are a part of his mission; the mission is a hush-hush affair. Maybe that's the reason he hid them here. Perhaps he didn't want to alarm me. If he needs these tools in his project, why hasn't he taken them with him? Maybe he doesn't need them today. Or perhaps these are his spare tools. It looks like Jacob and his colleagues are after an illegal treasure hunt!* She tried analyzing alone and tried answering all her questions, but it was all like squashing water, as she anyways had no guts to clarify her doubts from Jacob. She hurriedly zipped the bag and placed it back as before, hidden among the herbs and shrubs. She couldn't wait for Jacob to return to the cabin.

Being troubled by a surge of demoralizing emotions, she felt like she needed to relax and decided to take a swim in the lake. After she swam in the lake using all her best strokes, she felt better to some extent. That way, she tried to cope with her stress.

Whatever is bound to happen will happen with my life and my love towards Jacob. She floated flat on the water with her face towards the sky, her hands spread out on the water. With her eyes closed, she tried to calm down her mind. *I just know that I love Jacob. I simply need to hunker down in here without much fuss,* she ultimately realized. *I have to be loyal to him. I must always wish well for him; that's it.* She prayed to God to keep him safe. After some time, her anxiety diminished, and she felt relieved, ready to face anything that came her way if that was for Jacob's welfare.

That evening, when Jacob returned from his errand, he looked exhausted. She ran to welcome him with open arms and kissed him on his cheeks.

'I missed you, Jacob,' she said, concerned. 'I can't believe that it could have been so tough waiting for your return today. Did you have a good day?' she asked. Jacob was confused by Olivia's anxious behaviour.

'Of course, it was a great day, Olivia. What's the matter? Are you OK?' Jacob asked, returning her kiss. She brought him coffee as he slumped heavily on the couch.

'I am fine. Are you OK, Jacob?' asked Olivia solicitously, looking at his tired face. He nodded his head as a gesture to indicate he was fine. Jacob said he wanted to have an early dinner to immediately rest after that as he had had a long day. She made him dinner. The menu included fish, chips and green salad. By the time she'd finished preparing dinner, he had freshened up and was waiting by the dinner table.

'Olivia, how did you spend your time at the cabin today?' asked Jacob as he put a bite of his grilled fish into his mouth, with a fork. 'You look quite anxious.'

'Nothing much, Jacob,' said Olivia. Even though she had too many questions to ask, she felt she could not ask him anything because she was worried she might vex him by breaking his rule. Moreover, Olivia didn't want to upset Jacob in any way. Still, she felt desperate and impulsive.

'Jacob, I am a little worried today,' she finally said.

'I have ensured you that you would be safe here, Olivia,' Jacob said as he looked at her face with concern. 'Please tell me what else I need to do to make you feel safer?' he asked, caringly picking up her hands in his.

'It's not about that, Jacob,' said Olivia. 'I don't know whether I am allowed to ask you about this. Today, while I strolled in the backyard, I happened to see a green bag hidden among the shrubs- quite a big one.' She looked anxiously at him as if to study his expressions in reaction to her statement, and continued: 'I'm worried that someone might be stalking you. Remember? Yesterday night I also heard queer thudding and hammering sounds? So I thought maybe you are in danger or maybe you are being spied by someone,' she confessed and continued. 'Inevitably, I also overheard your conversation this morning with the two horsemen.' She studied his expressions again, and when she did not find any hostile look on his face, she said, 'I picked a book from your belongings this morning and saw a map in it. Of course, I was feeling bored and wanted to read a book, that's all. I did not mean to sneak at your things. I impulsively unfolded the map, and it looked like an old map of these mountain ranges with several red and green marks on it. So I kind of felt anxious. I know I shouldn't be asking anything about you and your errands. Pardon me, but I am just informing you of the reason for my anxiety and worry. I don't mean to ask any questions to you. I just felt concerned, that's all,' she said everything she had to say. Then sat silently, staring anxiously at his face.

He was listening to her intently but showed no expressions of anger or hostility, instead, smiled at her, 'OK, go on, what else you've got to say?' he asked, and she felt more confident to talk further.

'I don't know if these things which I encountered today are concerned with your safety or not. I just wanted to alert you because I want you to be safe,' Olivia explained as Jacob kept looking at her earnestly, smiling.

'Olivia, you don't want to mind your own business, do you?' He patted on her cheek, tenderly with love. They finished their dinner. He asked her to come into the bedroom. As she came inside, he held her in his arms and said, 'I know how to protect myself and you. You don't have to worry.'

'Jacob, I am not bothered about my safety. I am worried about yours,' she said innocently, placing her palms on his chest.

'Oh, really?' he chuckled. 'Why are you worried about my safety? I am a stranger to you. More than your safety, why are you concerned about mine?' he asked with a naughty look in his eyes.

'Jacob, you're not a stranger to me. I feel like I have known you all my life. You have been so kind to me. You have made me feel safe and secure. I think I love you and I want you to be safe always.' Olivia confessed, looking intently deep into his eyes.

He bent forward and nuzzled the tip of her nose with his. 'You are a silly little girl. Don't be anxious because everything is just fine. Nobody is going to hurt me. And yes, the green bag is mine, while everything is under control,' he kissed her lightly on her forehead.

He slowly pulled away from her embrace, went to his cupboard and brought out the book that contained the map. He took her on to the couch in the living room. He opened the map and said to her. 'You are not as innocent as I think of you, Olivia. Why should you feel anxious by seeing this map?' he asked in a challenging tone.

'Jacob, it looks like, it is a map of these mountain ranges and the marks on it in red and green indicate they might be some landmarks of value. So I guessed they might be landmarks for a hidden treasure or something like that. I just guessed because I am not a small child not to understand anything OK? Moreover, I inevitably overheard your conversation this morning and knew this whole thing you guys are up to was something against the law, though I don't know for sure whether it is about a treasure hunt,' she explained. She looked at him solicitously and requested, 'Please don't be angry with me....' she said, and he laughed out loud.

'Olive, you are intelligent and right about the map but wrong about something. You know that?' he asked, looking at her with soft eyes. She panicked a bit and looked at him nervously, trying to analyze what was she wrong about. She looked at him, fearing he would instruct her to pack her things immediately.

'You are wrong about the fact that I could be angry with you,' he chuckled. 'But just by seeing the map, how could you guess I'm after a hidden treasure? The map could have been some waste paper not of much use, right?!' he asked with a mocking suspicion, looking still amused. It was time for her to confess again.

'I saw the tools in the green bag hidden in the backyard among the shrubs. That confirmed my doubts.'

'OK! Got you! So you sneaked into the green bag!' he mocked at her teasingly, trying to pull her leg and making her feel guiltier, but both knew he was kidding.

'Jacob, I am truly sorry. I did not mean to sneak. I just felt impulsive, just in case there was something in the bag that was dangerous. I had to make sure that you were out of any danger because I feel obliged to protect you as you have been protecting me.' He was surprised by the way she justified her explanation.

'Good God!' he said, smiling. 'You are something. Do you know that? No problem. As you are staying here with me, you are bound to know about my mission sooner rather than later. Yes, I am here on a treasure hunt, and it's a secret mission. Better keep it to yourself. And I don't feel like sending you away from me at the moment. I think I like you a lot as well. And keep in mind that both of us are safe here,' he assured, giving her an adoring look. She felt relieved and hugged him as he tightly held her in his arms. She felt more secure than ever and wished they could always remain safe, happy and together, forever.

CHAPTER 5
~~~~~ ☐ ~~~~~

'Olivia, I'm going down the mountain, to the town of Wimberley this morning,' said Jacob early the next morning. 'I'm leaving right away. Do you need anything from the town?' he asked.

'Oh, Jacob, it's quite early. You haven't even had breakfast yet!' saying so, she hurried towards the kitchen.

'No worries, Olivia,' said Jacob. 'I cannot have breakfast this early. I'll eat later in a restaurant downtown. I need to set off at the earliest because I'll have to take a crosscut route through White River to reach the town faster. The river starts flowing vigorously after sunrise due to the melting of ice from the glaciers as it is mid-summer. So I should cross the river when it's flowing low in the early hours of the morning. You didn't tell me if you needed anything from the town.' He reminded her again.

'OK yes, I need a bath-towel and a pair of jogging shoes I guess,' she said biting her tongue lightly, harking back to how she'd stolen his chattel, and looked at him with guilt.

'OK fine, why not?' he said, patting her right cheek lightly, feigning anger. 'See you in the evening. I have a big day today. So you,... do not sneak into anything else out here; better mind your own business and know that you are safe. You know that right?' he asked her, mounting astride on Thunder while she nodded her head up and down, meaning yes.

Jacob had a meeting with his associates and two local men in the town that day, who would assist and guide them with the treasure hunt on Mount Jett. Peter had found the two eligible local men for the job, who had promised to aid them with searching, locating, as well as, digging for excavation, if necessary. They would carry out their mission in secret, by taking the two local men into their confidence. Before starting with the project, they still had some homework to do.

Jacob trotted on his horse down the hill through many rugged pathways, enjoying the jungle's beautiful scenery, the sunrise and the snow-capped mountains all around him. Thunder was an efficient stallion and carried Jacob effortlessly, through many steep mountain areas with confident balance, without budging from his track. Thunder helped Jacob cross the low White River without much difficulty.

When Jacob reached the restaurant in the town of Wimberley, he alighted from the horse, tied the stallion on to a hitching rail, walked inside and saw Peter seated with two other men in one corner of the atrium. Peter stood up and welcomed Jacob. He then introduced the two local men, Adrian and

Darby, to him. Adrian and Darby doffed their hats to Jacob while he greeted them with a welcoming gesture.

'Jacob, as you know, Wolfe, the middleman, had instructed to find some trustworthy local men to help us with the project,' said Peter looking at Adrian and Darby. 'And here they are to meet you. I talked to them yesterday about our project. They are good guys and keen as mustard, to be part of our team,' he said, and the two guys nodded their heads in approval.

'I'm glad to meet you both,' said Jacob.

They waited for a while for Brayan to arrive. As Brayan entered the restaurant, they saw that he was accompanied by another guy in his early thirties and introduced him to the others.

'Hello everyone, this is Gilbert. He knows the mountains quite well, and he is the one I told you about, who offered to help us with the locations if he got paid,' said Brayan.

'OK, that's good,' said Peter. 'We have three local men to help us now. Let's fix a daily wage for all the three of them.' They decided on a daily pay for all the three local guys, Gilbert, Adrian and Darby.

Adrian and Darby already knew that this would be a treasure hunt as Peter had informed them and were excited about it. They had promised to keep this whole mission a secret, with the hope that they would undoubtedly get some share or any form of fortune if the mission went successful. With Peter and Jacob's permission, Brayan described their mission to Gilbert because the local men were better for the job as they knew the mountains quite well. Still, Jacob, Peter and Brayan would do all the planning and technical work. Gilbert was very excited about the mission and said he had been waiting for this opportunity all his life. He tried haggling by demanding a share in the treasure if the mission was successful.

'This project is coordinated and controlled by a mastermind called Roark. He is the one who will decide what remuneration you all would get,' said Peter strictly. 'For now, you'll have to be satisfied with the daily wage fixed for you. Trust me, Roark would reward you handsomely, if you remain true to your job without attempting at any form of swindling,' he warned. Gilbert thought for a while and agreed, thinking, something was better than nothing.

'Gilbert, if you were waiting for this opportunity, why didn't you try unveiling the treasure on Mount Jett, all these years? Anyway, you are a local, right?' asked Jacob, out of simple curiosity.

'Of course, I've attempted several times to chase the treasure,' said Gilbert. 'Not only I, but many of the local youth have also broken their necks, trying to find the treasure. You guys seem highly technical. So I surmise you have higher chances of getting your hands on the treasure. I was waiting to join in hands with someone like you. Anyway, this chase is not going to be any easier. If it were a mere walk in a garden, anybody would have found the treasure by now,' he said as if he knew all the hardships associated with the treasure hunt on Mount Jett.

'So, how do you think you guys could help us?' asked Jacob. Even before one of them could answer, Jacob continued, 'I've heard that an old witch is living in a village nearby and that she could give us some genuine information about the treasure. Do you guys know anything about her?' asked Jacob.

Gilbert looked a little uneasy, but Adrian talked this time, 'Yes, we know about the old witch, and everybody around here knows about her. The witch is more than 110 years old, and she is the oldest human being living in these regions and knows a lot about the mountains' secrets. She has majestic powers. All these years she was in good health, but she is bed-ridden for the past few weeks due to her deteriorating health. It is undoubtedly wise for you guys to consult her first before embarking with the endeavour.

The old witch is highly insightful. Till now, she has not told the mountain's secrets to anybody. She decided that almost all the men who approached her were not fit for the job of chasing this particular treasure on Mount Jett. She has been advising almost everyone not to go after it because she believes they could get hurt unless they are the right people. Many youths who turned a blind eye to her advice and set out to find the treasure, have been lost on the mountains and never returned. Many young people have tried threatening her into telling the details about the treasure, but she wouldn't care. Many people attempted offering to pay her well and assuring her she would get a handsome share in the treasure, but she wouldn't budge to that and said she was not after wealth.

Maybe you guys must try your luck with her. Few of her followers say that recently being bedridden with ill-health and her frailness, she has been murmuring something queer. It seems she said, "the time has come for the mountain to reveal itself". It seems she had visions about that. So, now that you guys are here, maybe you can take a chance with her. Perhaps you are the right people she was waiting for; Who knows? Moreover, she is on her death bed and might easily give away whatever she knows about the treasure. Everybody knows she is a credible source.

But one point of concern is that, if she says you are not the right people and advises you to drop the idea and quit the mission, you'll have to obey her. In case you ignore her advises and proceed with the task, you are bound to get hurt on Mount

Jett,' he warned confidently.

'Ok, this is quite interesting and hopeful as well,' said Jacob. But after thinking a while, he said, 'it's quite discouraging too. What if the witch says we are not the right people and advises us to quit? Anyway, now that we are already here let's try our luck. Remember?- "The time has come for the mountain to reveal itself," said Jacob, delighted. All smiled at his statement, but Gilbert looked a little disturbed.

'I know, I once met the old witch myself and she advised me not to try the mountains.' Gilbert said. 'She didn't even give me any details about the treasure or its history. I tried to get information myself by exploring the central library out here. Though I collected some information about the treasure's existence, I did not get any details about its location or what the treasure exactly contained. I ignored the witch's advice and tried exploring, climbing up the mountain, but only halfway. I soon lost my confidence because I was scared I might get lost like the others. So, I retreated and saved my life. The mountain ranges are vast and difficult. I didn't know where exactly to explore. There are rumours that the treasure is somewhere on Mount Jett's summit, which is impossible to reach. The summit is completely and thickly snow-capped. Some say, the treasure exists in some hidden caves on the mountain top, but nobody knows where the caves are and where the caves' entrance is. The caves might be filled and covered with hardened ice, years ago. Some say the treasure is at the base of one of the mountains but not sure which mountain. Technicians from the federal state tried all possible methods to find the treasure. They did find a few things and artefacts that were not of much value. Many of my friends who ignored the old witch's advice are buried on the glaciers. Now that you guys are new and look intelligent, I would like to join in hands with you, so that, maybe I can make some fortune for myself if we find the treasure,' he said.

But Gilbert was against the thought of them meeting up with the witch. 'You guys need not care about the witch and the silly secrets hidden in her heart. People believe in her because she has been the oldest creature living here, and she has visions. I hope, you guys are not superstitious to believe in the crap she says. If she says you guys are not good enough for the job, that is very demotivating and may alleviate your confidence level. That is what happened with me and many others who tried chasing the treasure,' warned Gilbert. But Adrian and Darby thought it was going to be easy if they got useful information from the old witch.

'I think we must give it a try. Let's meet the old witch and see what she says. With her support, we might spare ourselves from an ambiguous cat's cradle,' said Jacob, who was listening intently.

'But Jacob, what if she said we're not capable and advised us not to try the mountains?' asked Brayan with frustration. 'That would abate our true mettle and bring down all our zeal. It would be ridiculous and daunting to begin the mission, with hope against hope. It's far better if we kick off without meeting her,' he insisted.

But Jacob and Peter had decided to meet the old witch because exploring the mountains for the treasure was not easy to do without proper details. Even the little information extracted from the witch would greatly help their expedition. They were curious to know the secrets of the mountain. So they all finally decided to meet up with the witch the same day because they wanted to prevent the impromptu efforts through the enigmatic mountain terrains, without any prior knowledge about the treasure's location.

After having breakfast in the restaurant, all the six men left on their horses for the old witch's shack to a nearby village called Penridge.

'By the way, what's the old witch's name?' asked Peter.

'She's Glinda,' said Adrian.

It was a 20 miles ride. Adrian was ahead of everyone as he guided them through the route. They soon came to the village of Penridge, situated at the base of a huge cliff. They passed through the village to an isolated place full of huge rocky boulders in the outskirts but closer to the mountains' foothill.

'Where are you taking us, Adrian?' asked Peter with curiosity. 'We are almost outside the village now, and we don't see any house or a cabin around here. Where does the witch live?'

'She lives in a shack among the labyrinth of these huge boulders,' said Darby. 'We need to dismount from our horses and walk on foot to a certain distance to reach her shack leaving the horses behind. The horses might not be able to pass through the narrow complicated pathways among the boulders.'

They all dismounted and tied their horses to a few trees around there and started to walk through small serpentine lanes that sliced through the boulders. After a distance of 30 yards, they saw the witch's house, an old-looking shiel. Outside the shack, there sat a man of around 40 years old, dozing on a chair. He opened his eyes reluctantly when he heard voices approaching.

'What do you guys want?' he asked in an irritable voice. 'If you are here to know about the stupid treasure, you better get lost. My great grandmother Glinda is on her death bed and might die anytime sooner. Don't you dare bother her.'

Jacob used his common sense and said, 'Sorry to bother you, pal. We are here, not for the treasure,' said Jacob, 'instead, to meet Glinda and know about her welfare in person. Heard she is bed-ridden. She is the oldest living soul, and we would be honoured if you could let us see her?' he requested.

Adrian said that the guy sitting on the chair was Glinda's grandson, Richard. Listening to what Jacob said, Richard grumbled, 'Give me a minute, guys... I'll be right back.' Saying so, Richard went into the shack.

After about ten minutes, a lady in her thirties came out of the shack. Seeing six strange men, she hesitated a bit, but recovered soon enough and said, 'Hello, I'm Richard's wife, Sarah. Glinda is bed-ridden past three months. But you are lucky that she's still alive. Amazingly, since this morning, Glinda is looking lively. She managed to sit up on her bed and murmured that someone important was on his way to meet her and that she needs to talk to him. But I don't know who among you is that important person. Till yesterday, she had instructed us not to let anyone inside her room. But today, I don't know why she happened to change her mind. All of you can please come in, and Glinda will decide whom she wants to talk to.' Sarah moved aside, gesturing the men to enter the shack.

At least this much was quite promising and optimistic. All six men went in first to the living room, and then they were guided into a small ambient haven, lit with several colourful, fragrant candles. That haven was where Glinda, the old witch, was resting on her spooky bed. Her wand laid on a table beside her bed with many spell-books stacked haphazardly on a tea-pie. Her room appeared too entrancing and conjuring, with many worn-out books littered in one corner. There hung, bundles of herbs, tied upside down blocking the windows. Trinkets hung on the colourful printed walls with paintings and pictures of demons and angels.

When she saw the men, Glinda gestured Richard to help her sit up. Glinda looked as old as the mountain itself; her body all scrunched up. Though her grandson Richard helped her to sit up on her bed, her back was bent, and she brooded in front, observed intently with a staring look at all the strange men, while they sat on the carpet, at the foot of her bed. They did not know what to say and how to start the conversation with her. They kept silent, waiting for Glinda to speak.

Glinda stopped her gaze on Gilbert and said, 'I've seen you before, lad. I remember advising you not to venture on the mountains to chase the treasure. Why are you still here?' Gilbert was embarrassed by her statement and came down of his high horse. The others gestured and signalled him to go out.

'You too, you are not good enough either,' she said to Brayan. Brayan's face lost colour. He kind of felt insulted and offended. But there was nothing he could do to help himself. So, he went out, grumbling restlessly, trying hard to slake his anger.

Richard and Sarah also darted out of Glinda's room, obeying her gestures. Adrian and Darby were next to go out.

Jacob and Peter feared that she might shove them away as well. Surprisingly, she looked at Peter and said, 'You can stay.' Peter was glad. Jacob almost got up, ready to go out, when she waved at Jacob asking him to sit down as well and said, 'You are the right person for this job. I've been waiting for you for long. I knew you were coming to see me today,' she said to Jacob, and he was mesmerized and remained speechless trying to figure out whether he had heard Glinda right. 'I knew deep in my heart that someone genuine would come along before I took my last breath. I saw visions that you were on your way to meet me today and that I feel obliged to give away the details I know about the mountains. The time has come for the mountain to reveal itself. I did not want to die, taking in with me all my valuable knowledge about the treasure, into my grave. I'm glad that you are finally here, sitting right in front of me, in my old shack,' she said to Jacob with a neutral expression on her face.

Jacob and Peter looked at each other, delighted. 'I am thrilled and happy to meet you, Glinda. This is a pleasant surprise!' said Jacob. He picked up her hands into his. Her hands were dry and worn out, and felt like a skeleton, without any flesh left in them. He caressed her hands lovingly, kissing them softly. Glinda felt rejuvenated and revitalized. She looked at him with quenched eyes, as if she sincerely acknowledged him.

CHAPTER 6
~~~~~ ◊ ~~~~~

Glinda gazed at Jacob intently, scrutinizing him thoroughly. Her deep-set tired eyes gave Jacob a once-over, with a sharp, powerful glare. Jacob was staggered and stupefied by the sagacity and strength in her tiny eyes. Her eyes looked like vast, deep blue oceans, with many hidden mysteries and treasures. He saw her eyes oozing out some kind of magic spell on him that made him melt from within.

Gracious me! How magnetic and magical! Jacob looked at Peter, who also sat speechless and captivated. He was looking at Glinda and waiting for her to speak up, enraptured by the depth in her eyes. Though Glinda was all debilitated and in the concluding days of her life, her eyes said a million stories.

'I was waiting with bated breath for you to come and meet me,' she said to Jacob. 'I'm delighted that you lad is finally here.' She gestured Jacob to come closer, and he did. She wanted to say something into his ears. 'You know what?' she whispered into his ears, 'I feel so lucky today, and I know from the depth of my heart that you are the right person,' she confirmed. Jacob was overwhelmed and did not know how to react. He couldn't discern whether she was blabbering something due to her delirious condition or was perfectly oriented and telling the truth.

'Glinda, do you know why I am here?' asked Jacob, 'and what do you mean by I'm the right person for the job? I haven't told you anything as yet, about me and the reason for my visit,' he said, looking a bit iffy.

'Of course, I know why you are here. Though your meeting with me today is due to a fortuity, it is destiny as well, that is meant to be.' Glinda said positively but like a riddle. 'You are here to reveal the mountain of its hidden treasure. What are your names by the way?' She asked the duo.

Jacob felt a little strange. *If the old witch says she knows why I'm here, then she must know my name as well!* 'I am Jacob, and this is my associate, Peter,' introduced Jacob.

'Maybe I don't know you personally, Jacob, but I know your eyes,' she said. Jacob felt quirky and did not understand heads or tails of what she meant by that. *She might have only guessed about our hush-hush business of chasing the treasure as she'd guessed about many other people who have met her before with the same motive.*

'Ok, you are right. I'll keep it real,' Jacob said. 'We're here to know the details and niceties of the hidden treasure. At the same time, I am fascinated by the fact that you are more than a century old, the oldest soul living around here and unfortunately bed-ridden. So, I thought it better to see you before my task as it would give me a lot of strength to reveal the old mountains,' said Jacob. Glinda was glad.

'Ok, my lad, thank you for that. You are benevolent.' She observed him for a while and said, 'You look befitting and positive. The mission agrees with you completely. What do you know about Mount Jett?' she asked him to assess his prior knowledge about the treasure.

'I know very little, as little as whatever is there in the literary narratives and of course, a little information from the rumours,' said Jacob. 'I know that there was once a gangster who dwelt on this mountain. He possessed a lot of loot with him. There is a conviction that most of his loot was stashed somewhere in the heart of the mountain after his death, and remains unchartered. Many youths have tried to ferret this particular treasure but in vain. Even the government has failed in the enterprise, despite making the most available techniques and skilled men. This is all I know and nothing more. You said you consider me the right person to reveal the mountain of its hidden treasure; so can you enlighten me with ridgy-didge, confidential information?' he asked with great expectation.

'Of course, I can and I will. It is the only reason

I am alive till now, and feel so lively today,' said Glinda with an expression he couldn't understand. 'Undoubtedly, you're the person I was waiting for, and in fact, I was worried whether you would ever approach me at all, though I had visions of you approaching me. I'm all set to enlighten you with every detail I know. Whatever you already know is negligible and with that meagre knowledge, it is impossible to unveil the hidden treasure, regardless of your skills and intelligence. So I would like to touch on the matter further. Now listen to me, listen carefully to what I say and make proper use of it. I would die happy if you could find the treasure.' She went into a deep trance for fifteen minutes without uttering a word, while Jacob and Peter kept looking at her and at each other's faces waiting for her to continue. Her deathly silence made Peter worried, thinking she had already kicked the bucket even before giving away any valuable information.

Suddenly she spoke up as if she'd heard him. 'Don't worry; I'm still alive. I was only trying to recall my memory, closing my eyes. I will not die until your mission is complete. I've waited all these years. It's no big deal; I can wait a little longer.' Glinda said as if she could decide the time of her death. The two men looked at her, stunned. She ran her palm over Jacob's face to confirm his honesty and ingenuousness.

'This story happened 150 years back,' Glinda began. 'You are right about the gangster. A century and a half ago, these particular Spruce mountain ranges were occupied and sojourned by a hard-core gangster named Jett. He was popularly known as "Jungle Jett". Jungle Jett had started his career of burglary, right from his adolescence. By the time he reached his middle age, he had die-casted himself into a highly skilled and an expert hand in planned robberies. Jungle Jett robbed banks, museums, trains, jewellery shops and whatnot. He conducted every single heist with perfect planning and unparalleled skills, an ideal racket by an exemplary dacoit. Every time, he saw to it that his gang came out with great success. Though people of the villages down the mountains knew that he took refuge on these mountain ranges with his team, nobody knew exactly where. His active gang consisted of at least 35 to 40 people, including men and women. They were all like one big family.

Jungle Jett's wife was his childhood love, and her name was Georgina. Georgina was equally trained and skilful in that kind of job. The couple made a perfect pair. Soon after every burglary, they took refuge on these mountain ranges with their gang, for at least two to three months. They also doled out and distributed some of their loot to the poor people living in the foothill villages. People from the villages called him 'Jungle Jett' with love. They adored and worshipped him. Jungle Jett and Georgina had a daughter named Cynthia,' said Glinda. Jacob and Peter listened to her earnestly and gaped at her with tremendous surprise. It was hard to believe that she knew such minute details not available in any books or hearsay. They waited eagerly for the fascinating truth that was yet to come.

Glinda continued. 'As you know, Jungle Jett was a famous and popular gangster and ruled his reign as a burglar for nearly 40 years. So you can imagine how much wealth he must have stockpiled. The law enforcement officers tried to capture him many times but in vain. The village people were very protective of him and never gave any clue to the police about him and his lair. They always said they knew nothing about him. The mountain ranges have been so enormous that it was challenging for the police to apprehend him. He kept switching places on the vast cavernous mountains that made it even more unfathomable. Moreover, during those days, the police did not possess proper ammunition and automobiles to capture him easily.

Ultimately, Jungle Jett died in his late sixties, due to some chronic disease, without ever being seized by the police. After his death, his gang dispersed, carrying whatever wealth they could manage to take with them. His lovely wife Georgina was heartbroken after her beloved husband, Jett's death, and did not know what to do with all the loot and her enormous favourite jewellery she had. She dispensed some of it to the poor people, and she hid the remaining treasure in the heart of the mountain with the highest peak, which is now popularly called as "Mount Jett", after Jungle Jett's name. She left the mountain with her daughter and supposedly went off to a far land with the fear that she might get seized by the police and wished to come back sometime later. But somehow she never came back. So the treasure remains on Mount Jett. People think that it is a myth. But I know it is the truth.

It is the truth that there is a brass chest weighing around 300 lb. that contains gold ornaments, diamonds, precious stones, pearls and much other priceless jewellery worth eyeteeth. This chest with her favourite jewellery is hidden safely on Mount Jett. Government has tried hiring many archaeologists and detectorists to resume the treasure several times. They were able to unearth a few bits and bobs, here and there. Despite all sincere efforts, they could not recover the brass chest and do not know anything about where the brass chest of treasure is hidden. Since many years, people have just stopped looking for the treasure, thinking it is nothing but a general misbelief.

One more important thing that I would want to tell you is, though Jungle Jett was not a pious person, he believed in Buddha's principles. He was a kind-hearted person and helped the poor, believed in and led an uncomplicated personal life, with many devoted followers of his own. Jungle Jett only plundered wealth from the deceitful rich. He possessed an idol of Buddha, made in pure gold weighing 100 kgs which he had great sentiments for and considered the smiling golden Buddha idol as his lucky charm. Because the Buddha idol had a special place in his heart, the idol was buried after his death, along with his body, on the mountains 100 years back by his wife Georgina and her best friend Anna without anybody else's knowledge. Anna was a trustworthy friend and was Georgina's associate in every one of their missions.' Glinda sat, thinking deeply for some time in a brown study.

'Why did Georgina never come back for her hidden treasure?' asked Peter. 'Have you any idea about that?'

'Yes, I have,' said Glinda lying back slowly on her bed. She was tired of sitting, and her back hurt. Jacob helped her lie down while she continued, 'It's a good question Peter but did I say Georgina went away with her daughter, Cynthia? Oh no, I'm sorry, these days I have a confusing and poor memory. Georgina never went anywhere with her daughter. I believe that Georgina still dwells there on Mount Jett,' said Glinda and looked at the aghast faces of

Jacob and Peter who were not able to get the gist of her statement because Glinda's talks were full of puzzles.

'What do you mean by Georgina still dwells on Mount Jett? This is all so confusing?' exclaimed Peter. Glinda continued. 'Yes, it's confusing because everybody thought Georgina went away to a far off place with her only daughter, Cynthia. But Georgina did not want to quit the mountains. Only her daughter, Cynthia, went away to a far off land after marrying a handsome young man while Georgina stayed back in this village,' said Glinda.

Jacob and Peter looked at each other's faces with great confusion. 'Then where is Georgina now?' asked Jacob. The witch tried laughing at his statement, but she couldn't manage to laugh because she did not have the stamina, instead her expression was out of her control and turned into a funny grimace. 'For God's sake! You silly lad! When her husband, Jungle Jett died 100 years ago, Georgina was already in her late fifties. Where can she be now? She, of course, is dead,' said Glinda.

Jacob felt stupid for asking such a naïve question. 'Ok, if she never went away with her daughter, where did she stay- when and how did she die? And how do you know about all this?' Jacob had a series of questions in his mind and couldn't wait to get her answers. The old witch suddenly coughed, and Jacob immediately offered her some water.

She said she wanted to rest. Jacob felt guilty for asking her multiple questions at a time.

Glinda slept for a long time, and the duo sat there, waiting for her to wake up. She had stopped narrating the story in the spur of the moment when it was getting truly interesting. Jacob and Peter felt restless. Glinda's grandson, Richard, suggested that they go home and return the next day. But Jacob and Peter did not budge from their places by the foot of Glinda's bed. They wanted to know everything that Glinda had to say. For a moment, they even feared if she died without giving all the information. But somewhere in the depth of his heart, Jacob knew that Glinda would not ditch him. She had said she'd waited so long for his arrival. So he had the confidence that the old witch would not die without fulfilling her wish of telling him all the secrets she knew about Mount Jett.

Jacob was also worried that Olivia would be waiting for him to return before the sun went down. But the situation here at witch's shack was critical and inevitable. Listening to everything that Glinda had to say was the priority at the moment. So, Jacob decided that they stay back till Glinda woke up. Glinda slept for nearly ten hours, and the two men rested in her room, on a carpet on the floor after consuming the food that Richard offered. The four men waiting outside were on tenterhooks and thus went back to their respective abodes promising to meet the next day.

~ ~ ~ ~

'Jacob, wake up,' said Peter in the midnight, shaking Jacob, who was fast asleep at the foot of Glinda's bed. Jacob woke up with a start and was glad to see that the old witch was wide awake and sitting upright on her bed. She looked stable, buoyant and full of vim and vigour. Jacob was relieved to see that she was very much alive and still holding the essence of life in her skinny and crumpled little body. Jacob looked at his watch. It was past midnight. Richard's wife, Sarah, was tending to Glinda by feeding the old witch with some green vegetable soup. Half of the soup dribbled out of Glinda's mouth as she tried to swallow it down her emaciated, anorexic throat. Once Sarah was done feeding Glinda with the soup, she fed her with some water, wiped Glinda's mouth thoroughly and went back to the kitchen.

Jacob and Peter sat in front of Glinda like two school kids. Glinda slowly stretched her right arm and caressed Jacob's face. 'What is your name again?' She asked, looking at Jacob with love.

'I'm Jacob, Glinda. Do you feel strong enough to talk to us now? If not, we can wait for you till you feel better,' said Jacob with concern.

'How do you think I look, Jacob? I feel as strong as the mountain itself. By the way, where was I?'

she asked, trying to remember and resume the story she was narrating to them and wanted to get it off from her chest completely.

This time, Jacob thought it better, not to rush Glinda into answering his series of questions. 'Glinda, don't stress yourself. Take your time and tell me whatever you want to say to me. Can you tell me, if Georgina never went away with her daughter, where did she stay before she died?' he asked calmly.

Glinda cleared her throat. 'Georgina stayed with her best friend Anna right in this village, but in disguise. She did not want anyone to recognize her with the fear of being apprehended by the police. Georgina wanted to be closer to Mount Jett, where she had hidden her treasure and buried her husband's body. She could not stay longer in this village with Anna because of her tormenting depression. So, within a year of Jungle Jett's death, she went back to the mountain one fine day, saying she would join her husband. None saw her after that. She must have died sometime later on, on the mountains,' said Glinda. She closed her eyes for some time, and Jacob saw tears welling up in Glinda's eyes. He sat silent for some time.

After he confirmed that Glinda was feeling ok, he asked, 'If Georgina died, how can you say that she still dwells in the mountains, don't you think it's absurd?' asked Jacob.

The old witch smiled a secret smile and said, 'Of course she must have died long back, but when she was alive she was a strong spirited woman with a great passion for her work and their loot. So I see visions that her soul is restless and her spirit is guarding her treasure on Mount Jett,' she said confidently.

Jacob and Peter felt strange again because the story of Georgina's spirit being on guard of the treasure seemed like it was her delusion. But they could not deny it as they firmly believed that she was a credible source.

'Glinda, how do you know all about Georgina?' Asked Jacob.

'My dear boy, "how do I know?"...should not be your concern. Still, I want to tell you everything. Georgina's friend, Anna, was my MOTHER! I was born on Mount Jett. I was brought up on Mount Jett, till I came of age. Georgina had stayed in this village with us after her daughter, Cynthia left. She had taken refuge in this same shack of mine, in disguise, when I was a little girl!!

CHAPTER 7

~~~~~ 〇 ~~~~~

'Good heavens! What a marvellous story!' Exclaimed Jacob.

'My mother, Anna, was Georgina's bosom friend and her companion at work,' continued Glinda. 'My mother had worked alongside Georgina in almost all of their burglaries. When Jungle Jett took his last breath, I must have been somewhere around 12... 13.... or 14 years old maybe?... I don't remember what my age was then, exactly. I have seen Jungle Jett, Georgina and their daughter Cynthia from close because our families were in a cordial relation with each other. But, I just have a few memories of them, as I was small at the time. It all happened a long time ago. Whatever memory I had of them has faded with time.'

'Where is Georgina's daughter, Cynthia, currently?' asked Jacob, 'Did you ever hear from her after she left with her husband? Is she alive?'

Glinda tried to recall by taking a trip down her memory lane and said, 'I suppose not, Cynthia was at least 15 to 16 years elder to me. So it is not likely that she could be alive now. After she got married and went away with her husband, she had once written a letter to her mother, saying she was happy and that she had changed her name to be detached from her parent's burglary history.

That was it. We never heard from Georgina's daughter any time later; also never heard from Georgina after she left our shack and went back to the mountain,' said Glinda, feeling nostalgic. Jacob and Peter were enthralled by listening to Jungle Jett and Georgina's real story. The fascinating fact was that Glinda was a couple's contemporary and knew them well.

It was almost dayspring by the time Glinda finished narrating the story. 'Before I take my last breath, I want you to scout up and bag the treasure, because, I firmly believe that this is the right time,' said Glinda to Jacob. 'I know the location where Jungle Jett's body was buried on the mountain, along with the smiling golden Buddha idol. When Georgina was burying his body, my mother Anna helped her with the task, aided by a few other reliable members of the gang. I was with my mother at that moment and witnessed the whole conduct of burial and last rites. It was a soul-stirring event, which I cannot forget till today. I saw them burying Jungle Jett's body along with the smiling golden Buddha idol, at the mid of timberline on the north face of Mount Jett. Suppose you excavate exactly in that area of the timberline on the north face of Mount Jett, for which I can give you a landmark, you are sure to find the golden Buddha idol with studs of diamonds fixed on Buddha's gold attire,' she said as if everything had come back to her, crystal clear.

Jacob and Peter were left spellbound by the anecdote they'd just heard. 'Great! That's one part of the treasure. But, what about the brass chest full of precious jewellery?' asked Peter. 'Do you know where it is stashed?'

'Of course, I know. My mother gave me that information before she died in her eighties. But, cautioned me not to give away the information to anyone unless I found the right person. I am a born witch, and my mother believed in me and my visions,' Glinda justified.

'Where is the chest then?' implored Jacob. 'I want to unearth it before you decide to end your worthy life. I want to prove my worth to you because I feel like I'm in the seventh heaven. After all, you considered me as a promising person, but why do you consider me worthy of the job, is a mystery to me. But anyway, I'm flattered and felicitous, thank you,' he said.

'Don't you worry, my boy,' Glinda tried to soothe him. 'Nothing's gonna happen to me until you reveal the mountain, off its treasure. The brass chest of treasure is stashed in the caves, at the base of Mount Jett's summit. The elephantine caves are covered with snow and ice and have transformed into mighty, robust glaciers in the past century and a half. Nobody knows the exact location of the hidden caves around here except me because, I am the only living soul right now who resided in those caves once upon a time,' confided Glinda.

She picked up her conversation, 'Now I feel so very relieved and released off, of the burden on my chest. I am relieved that I enlightened you about the mighty hidden caves and their exact location. But now you have a greater responsibility of finding the caves in propria persona, only after which, you can find the treasure. No one from this current generation knows where the caves exist. These caves are reverberant and alveolate beyond your imagination. When Jungle Jett's gang dispersed after his death, the caves remained abandoned and transmuted into hard glaciers. The caves have many secret places, and now your job is first to locate the probable site of the caves and explore them to find the treasure. The caves are located at the base of the summit, and their entrance is on the east face of Mount Jett,' said Glinda confidently.

Jacob and Peter were incredibly pleased because Glinda had revealed both the brass chest and Buddha idol's locations. This information was crucial to proceed with the mission, instead of blindly trying to empty the sea with a thimble.

'I need to answer your other question, why I consider you worthy of the job. I know that you are the right person because I just know it,' said Glinda. 'I'm a witch and have the powers. My powers have grown stronger over the years. I have seen you in my visions and had a sixth sense that you were coming to see me. Now I'm convinced because I saw your worth in person, in your eyes,' she justified looking deep into Jacob's eyes.

'And what about Peter?' asked Jacob. 'Why did you let him stay back with me while you narrated the story?'

'In your mission, you need at least one trustworthy associate, a partner. When I studied all the men who came with you, I knew Peter was the only one you could count on, and so I allowed him to stay back and listen to the story and the desired information. I feel that Peter could be true to his job and of great help to you in your intense chase for the treasure. I know it by looking at his eyes. It is my responsibility not only to convey you the details but also to protect and safeguard your interests in this mission,' she ensured.

'What about the other men who came with me? Are they all unreliable?' asked Jacob. Glinda thought for a while and seemed a little confused. Jacob could not read her mind because of her variable expressions.

'The other men…,' she said, 'I'm not so sure about their loyalty. I saw some raggle-taggle mixed emotions and motives in their eyes. But one thing I can assure you is that it's all right if you want to take their assistance in finding and unearthing the treasure. But once you recover the treasure, you need to be very careful with those men,' she cautioned.

'No worries about that, Glinda,' said Peter. 'We're all working for a Kingpin by name, "THE ROARK", and he would see to it that we all do our jobs sincerely. He has spies all over us, and nobody would dare to cheat on him,' justified Peter.

'THE ROARK? A kingpin? Ok, whatever! He is not my concern,' shrugged Glinda. 'I've done my job, and I am relieved of the burden off my shoulders. Once you resume the chest and the idol, it's up to you what you will do with it. I certainly know that I have done the right thing at the moment. Once you find the treasure, protecting it is your responsibility. I can only caution you. How you are going to manage that is none of my business.

You shouldn't be wasting any more of your valuable time now. You must swing into action right away. First try to dig for Buddha idol as I'm sure of its location because I had seen it when it was buried, with my very own eyes. Still, I feel that you might face some problem with retrieving the idol and I do not know what the problem could be,' said Glinda and sat quietly, thinking deeply for some time. She looked worried.

'Glinda, what is it? You look disturbed,' asked

Jacob with concern.

'There is one big hindrance, Jacob,' said Glinda, looking restless. 'It is Georgina's spirit, the one and only Georgina, Jungle Jett's wife and Cynthia's mother. Georgina's spirit is guarding the treasure. I get visions of her spirit on Mount Jett, wearing a diamond necklace to which the key to the brass chest is fastened. That's why I said Georgina still dwells on the mountain; though not in person, her soul dwells. She could be one hell of a demon right now who might pose problems with your treasure hunt,' said Glinda.

'So, what do we do now?' asked Peter. 'How can we go about the mission without getting hurt?'

'Do not worry. There might be a solution. It depends on whether Georgina's spirit likes you or not. If you can make her spirit happy, she might calm down and make your endeavour easier,' said Glinda with hopes.

'How can I please her spirit? Is there any remedy you can suggest that could make her spirit come to terms with me?' asked Jacob, thinking, the theory of Georgina's spirit guarding the treasure was something paradoxical and untrue.

'Jacob, something tells me that you do not believe in the existence of Georgina's spirit. You must know that she was a strong-willed woman. Her love towards Jungle Jett was immense, and her passion for all the treasure you want to find was substantial. She even had a tattoo on her forearm with Jett's name. So her spirit has been guarding the treasure for long and wouldn't let it go, so easily. You need to trust in the existence of her spirit genuinely; only then you can make her happy; only then she may pose no obstacles in your efforts.' Glinda advised.

Jacob looked aghast at Glinda, realizing her powers in reading his mind. *Good God! Glinda has some real powers. Right, I indeed thought the story of Georgina's spirit was crap. I'm sorry, I need to trust Glinda, her story and the existence of Georgina's soul, though it's the most challenging thing to tame my mind into believing in something supernatural,* he thought.

'Do not worry, it's not your fault,' said Glinda to Jacob. 'It's the fault of this modern scientific world and your generation that you deny believing in the existence of spirits. So I genuinely suggest that you first need to build the confidence within you and trust in the existence of Georgina's spirit. Only then can I help you to calm down her spirit,' she said, touching his hair with her skeleton-like fingers, examining some hidden meaning in them. 'Today, you can go back,' she permitted, 'and make your mind up, to trust in Georgina's spirit, which you can accomplish by your will power and meditation.

Tomorrow, you'll have to embark on the journey to find Buddha idol. After you retrieve the Buddha idol and only after you develop complete trust in the existence of Georgina's spirit, come back to me. I'll guide you with the further proceedings and will suggest you a remedy to simmer down Georgina's soul, so you will not face any obstacles in the venture to bag the brass chest of treasure,' instructed Glinda.

'I'll mark down everything you said to me. I will sincerely follow your instructions,' ensured Jacob and saw a glint of unexplained happiness, in Glinda's eyes.

It was already late in the morning. Jacob and Peter thanked Glinda and bid her goodbye after wishing her good health and promising to follow all her suggestions.

Jacob suddenly remembered Olivia and felt concerned that she must have been restless all night, all alone in the cabin on the mountains. Even though he did not know that he would be staying at Glinda's the previous night, he felt guilty for leaving Olivia alone.

After bidding farewell to Glinda, Jacob did some shopping for Olivia and hurried back to the cabin because he felt the urge to see her at the earliest. He wanted to hug her for all the good things that were happening to him. Jacob decided that Olivia was his Goodluck figurine. He felt that something genuine in her could make his life complete and was ecstatic to return to her.

~ ~ ~ ~

Olivia was extremely relieved when she saw Jacob approaching on Thunder. She was sitting in the porch with a coffee mug in her hand, anticipating his arrival. As soon as she saw him, she rose from her seat, kept the cup down on the chair, didn't care when some of the coffee spilt, hurried towards him exhilarated.

As Jacob dismounted the stallion, she ran to him, and the duo hugged each other with a compassionate smack. After they kissed and cuddled, Olivia remained silent, hugging him without asking any questions. She was aware that he had gone to the town on an important task and thought it was against the rule to ask him anything about it. She was delighted that he was here, back with her at the moment, which was all she'd wished for through the previous night.

They stood embracing each other for few minutes and Jacob broke the silence, 'I'm so sorry, Olivia,' he said brushing his lips against the tip of her nose, 'Yesterday when I left, I was not aware that it would take me so long. But it was all worth it, and I am thrilled with all the proceedings that took place. At the same time, I beg your pardon, to have left you all alone here, all through the night,' he confessed.

'Jacob, definitely I was worried about you all night long. But deep in my heart, I knew that you would return, as soon as you finished your work in town. Of course, I missed you a lot, but now that you are here, I'm very much delighted. You don't have to give me any explanation for returning late. It's truly fine.' Olivia said, placing both her palms on his chest and looking intently into his soft brown eyes, that emitted immense affection.

He felt pleased with her positive thinking and accepting nature. He somehow thought that she was trustworthy and could make the best companion for his life. The duo went into the cabin, holding each other. He freshened up. While they had breakfast, he felt impulsive to tell her about the previous day's events because he was very excited about it all. He briefly told her about the encounter with the old witch, Glinda and the vital information she gave him. Olivia was amazed that Jacob was telling her all this. She felt great to see that he was divulging sensitive information to her about his mission and so comfortably confiding in her.

'Jacob, I am very happy for you. Even I want to contribute something towards your mission. I would die to do anything to make your mission successful,' she said, holding his hands. He felt relaxed in her homey company.

'Did you know any of this story about Jungle Jett, before?' Jacob asked her just out of curiosity.

'Oh yes, a little of course,' she said. 'As you know, I'm a girl from Figlington, a village down the mountain; I have been hearing stories since my childhood, about this gangster Jungle Jett and his burglaries. I could connect with the story Glinda narrated to you. But, not heard anything about Georgina and their daughter, Cynthia. Of course, nothing about Anna and her relation to Glinda. So whatever Glinda told you is a piece of fantastic information.

I've heard about Glinda, the old witch, and that she knows a lot about the treasure and that she has been very strict about not giving away the details to anyone. I'm so very proud of you because she considered you as a promising person for the job and gave away her secret piece of information to you, among the lot. This is great news to me, and I'm thrilled for you,' Olivia said with raised spirits. She then carried all the dishes to the sink to wash, and Jacob helped her with the same.

'What are your plans for today?' She asked.

'I do not have any particular plan for today, but there is one important thing, of course,' said Jacob. 'I need to focus my mind into believing that Georgina's spirit exists because Glinda said, only then she could help me to proceed with the project. So now, after a bit of catnapping, I will go by the lake and do some meditation and try to focus my mind, as far as possible,' he said.

'Yeah, that's a good idea.' Olivia concurred. He took a nap after feeding the stallion with hay and water. In the afternoon, he went by the lake and did some meditation, with a reverent concentration on believing and trusting in Georgina's spirit. After some time, he started to feel focused and connected with nature, its miracles and mysteries.

When all these miraculous things on earth are real, the existence of Georgina's spirit is real as well. Man has limited powers, and he can sense things only with his restricted mind and sensations. Undoubtedly, there are many things in this universe, beyond the ability of human perception. Spirits and souls of the dead could be as alive as human beings, and there could be a virtual world of spirits and souls as well, a life after death, which humans cannot perceive all the time but do sometimes, who knows? Maybe Glinda has the power to visualize Georgina's spirit. She must be talking to the spirit as well, in her visions.

'I trust in your existence, Georgina. I feel good to trust in your soul. I am experiencing a strange feeling of being close-knit with you,' murmured Jacob. *'I can feel the vibes of your presence. You have been an intense person throughout your life. Your body must have perished, but not your soul or your passions,'* he said aloud without his knowledge. His will power

was strong that helped him to concentrate. After an hour or so, he felt confident about his belief.

In the evening, Jacob and Olivia sat in the porch, sipping coffee, watching the blissful sunset as usual. 'Olivia, now that I have told you everything about my mission that it's a private underworld effort and that I'm one of the major culprits in this mission, hope you will not turn me in with the police!' Jacob made a facetious comment, feigning fear in his eyes.

'Jacob, it's a poor joke. You know I love you. Don't you? I would never do anything that would bring harm to you. In fact, I want to do whatever I can, to be of some help in your mission, to make it successful. One thing I'm worried about is your safety, though. I want you to be very careful because the mission is against the law.' Olivia cautioned solicitously.

'I'm sorry for my poor joke but don't you worry, honey. I'll be on my toes and will play it safe,' assured Jacob. 'Moreover, I do not want you to get involved in my mission because I do not want you to risk your life,' he said firmly.

Olivia felt warm in her heart, with all the care and concern he bestowed upon her. Even though he had never said that he loved her, she saw his love in his eyes, actions and words. She wanted to kiss him and wondered if Jacob felt the same way. She decided to give the thought a rest because he was here on a critical mission, and she did not want to distract him in any way.

'Jacob, I have never seen such love and affection in my life. Please consider me in your mission. I would give anything to bring you happiness,' she confessed. He hugged her deep and remained that way for a long time. That night as he lay on the couch, he thought of his ex-girlfriend Sophia, who was no more. Tears filled his eyes unknowingly. He felt confident within, about everything happening at the moment in his life; with Glinda, Olivia, Georgina, and of course, about the hidden caves and the treasure. He soon fell asleep, hoping for the best days ahead. He dreamt of Buddha idol as if the virtuous idol was already in his possession and that he would be lucky in the coming days.

~ ~ ~ ~

Olivia was woken up in the midnight by the thudding and hammering sounds again. She came out of the cabin and looked around. The sounds were indistinct concerning their directions. She felt agitated. She went to the cliff's edge in front of the cabin and looked down towards the village right at the cliff's bottom. Sounds came like waves carried by the wind as if they were coming from afar. With a keen lookout, she assessed that they were coming from the cabin itself or maybe from behind the cabin somewhere. She hurried to the cabin's backyard to the place where she'd seen the big green leather bag of tools among the shrubs. But to her astonishment, the green bag was missing.

Gosh! Where's the green bag? Jacob said it was his bag. He is fast asleep on the couch. Who else could be working with the tools from the bag? Could it be his work partners? These creepy sounds are freaking me out. I couldn't even make out from where the sounds are coming. This is absurd, ridiculous! For a moment, she thought of waking Jacob but decided against it because she did not want to disturb his Godly sleep. *He needs to have an unflustered goodnight sleep to get enlivened by tomorrow morning, to embark on his mission. It would be selfish if I tried waking him up just because of my silly illusions.* Thinking so, she went back to the cabin and looked at the couch. When she saw his faint figure in the moonlight, sleeping tight, she went to the bedroom and settled herself back on the bed, but couldn't sleep for the next one hour and a half, so kept tossing and turning.

The sounds had stopped. Even then, Olivia couldn't sleep a wink because she was freaked out and feeling worried. To pass her time, she started to read Mount Jett's history from one of Jacob's collection of books. She read about Jungle Jett and was surprised to know about the popularity of the gangster among the village folks. Nothing was mentioned about his wife Georgina or his actual abode on the mountain. Olivia guessed that Jungle Jett had kept his dwelling and his family, a secret from the general population throughout his life.

She recalled the story narrated to Jacob by Glinda. She was amazed by knowing about Georgina's skills and expertise in burglary, despite being a woman. She also felt fascinated by Georgina's intense and impeccable love towards Jungle Jett. Olivia felt very sorry for Georgina, remembering how she was heartbroken after her husband's death and how she was utterly lost and deprived of all her energy and enthusiasm, even with her supporting friends and gang around her.

Olivia was surprised by the strength of love in one's life. *Individually we are all nothing. We all need someone to love us and someone we could love in return, to make us feel vital and alive.* Olivia decided that she would be there for Jacob all his life, whether he accepted her or not. She decided to serve him till her last breath. She knew that she loved him truly and deeply and was ready to sacrifice her life, serving and helping him. The weird sounds had stopped long back, and it was almost daybreak. Out of curiosity, she went to the backyard again to see the green tool bag and was surprised to see that the bag was back there, safe and sound.

Brilliant! She felt stupid because she couldn't

understand what was happening around there. She'd thought there was no one around the cabin except Jacob and herself. But she was proved wrong. *Maybe, my crazy intense love for Jacob has rendered me insane. I need to pull myself together and relax my thoughts*, she decided.

When she came back into the cabin, she faintly saw Jacob moving on the couch. He writhed in pain. She assessed that he was suffering from pain in his body and limbs due to his strenuous and laborious schedules. He was sleeping on his flat abdomen with his face turned to the opposite side. She sat by his side on the couch and pressed his legs and massaged his back, spine and shoulders, slowly with her palms and fingers, applying perfect pressure to make him feel relaxed, to remove any kind of pain and negative energy from his system. The acupressure and kneading on his muscles gave him great comfort.

After some time, he tossed around to face her, partially opened his eyes and looked at her lovingly. He felt good and dozed with relief while she smiled and continued to press his legs. Unexpectedly, he pulled her towards him in a cosy embrace, and she fell on his neck. 'Never mind Olivia, I'm fine, really,' he said and went back to sleep, embracing her. Snuggling and canoodling at the dayspring, the duo fell asleep, free from all anxiety, pain and apprehension, following a bout of mindfulness.

CHAPTER 8
~~~~~ ☐ ~~~~~

Jacob, Peter and Brayan were the three men assigned by Roark, for the job of chasing the treasure on Mount Jett. It was only Jacob and Peter, to whom Glinda had narrated Jungle Jett and Georgina's complete story and given significant details about the treasure. Jacob and Peter sensed that it would be unfair to keep Brayan in the dark from all this information because Brayan was an essential member of Roark's mission too. Moreover, all of them were under Roark's supervision. So, they would not dare to keep everything a secret from Brayan. Glinda had assured them that they could include the other four men in the mission. Still, she had cautioned about them.

Next morning, all the six men met by the White River. Brayan, Gilbert, Adrian and Darby were very curious to know about the information that was given to Jacob and Peter by the old witch.

'Hey there, Jacob. Would you mind telling us what the old witch said to you?' asked Brayan.

'Of course not, I would be happy to appraise you with all the details about Mount Jett because we are all here to work together in harmony. We need each other's sincere assistance to make the mission successful,' said Jacob. He then narrated to them the story of Jungle Jett, his wife Georgina, and her spirit on guard of the treasure. 'The bonus information that we got from Glinda is about the golden Buddha idol that weighs 100 kg. The idol could be found at the mid of timberline on Mount Jett's north face. Today we will locate the spot with the equipment we have. If we could pinpoint the location sooner with time to spare, we can even start digging and excavating for the idol today itself. Glinda also gave us information about the brass chest weighing 300 lb., which is full of jewellery made of gold, diamonds and precious pearls and stones. The brass chest is ostensively hidden somewhere in the caves at the base of the summit,' said Jacob. For the time being, Jacob thought it better not to mention about the caves' entrance that it was on the east face of Mount Jett. Jacob also didn't utter that Georgina had taken refuge in Glinda's shack after Jungle Jett's death and anything about their only daughter, Cynthia. He thought that information was nowhere concerned with their treasure hunt. He did not mention anything about Anna and her relation to Glinda as well.

The other men were stunned, listening to momentous, valuable information given by Glinda. Still, Gilbert was not completely happy with the information received. He asked doubtfully, 'Everybody knows that there are hidden caves on Mount Jett and a treasure is hidden in the caves. Now we know what we are searching for; a brass chest of treasure and a Buddha idol. Of course, we know where to find the idol now. But just this information is not enough. We still don't know where and in which direction the caves' entrance is located to find the brass chest of treasure! We can't just beat around the bush to locate the caves. We need information about where exactly the entrance to the caves is located. Moreover, Georgina's spirit, ghost and things like that, are all hooey and nonsense,' he said hopelessly.

'Relax, Gilbert. Don't be forlorn,' said Jacob, 'Glinda said that the demon in Georgina's spirit is guarding the brass chest. We need to believe in the existence of her spirit; her soul. Only then Glinda can help us proceed with the brass chest hunt. If we fail to trust in Georgina's spirit, Glinda said she would be rendered helpless. I have tried my best to focus on the existence of Georgina's soul and her energy, and now I ultimately believe that Georgina's soul endures and is guarding the treasure on the mountain. I wish you all do the same as well.

Glinda has instructed me to see her again only after we recover the Buddha idol, and only after we genuinely come to believe in Georgina's spirit. So, for now, we'll have to set off to look for Buddha Idol and not worry about the brass chest or the cave entrance,' concluded Jacob and everybody agreed, nodding their heads in accord, as they had no other choice but to trust in and follow Glinda's instructions.

Jacob and his associates had brought their equipment with them. Jacob possessed a high-end metal detector and a compass and many other tools required for the job. He was highly skilled in such errands and had roughly come to mark the probable spots on the map approximately, even before Glinda's information. Past one month, he had been studying Mount Jett with its history and its terrains, as far as possible, which he believed could make things easier when the actual project commenced. They also had all the things needed for a little mountaineering, for their expedition on the mountain. Jacob and Peter were also trained with mountaineering and mining technical skills and had all the gears associated with it.

'I am well versed and quite familiar with the mountains,' Gilbert said. 'I was born and brought up here, down in the village and have ventured several times to climb on to the summit. Only once was I able to reach the base of the summit but never the peak. Reaching the peak is out of the question, as it is baroque and needs real mountaineering skills and good luck,' he said.

'You need not worry about the base or peak of the summit for now,' said Jacob. 'For today, let us concentrate on the timberline alone, that too the one on the mid of north face of Mount Jett. Let's take one pursuit at a time.' he advised.

'Ok then, that's cool,' agreed Gilbert because he couldn't even imagine climbing on to the base of the summit but kept boasting that he knew the mountains very well. They studied the map, started their journey on horses, towards their port of call, the timberline, at the mid of the north face, as guided by the compass.

They had to pass through the mountain's wilderness to reach the timberline almost at the height of 10,000 ft. from sea level. It was one heck of a journey. As it was mid-summer, they didn't have to worry about snow and ice to reach the timberline. They had guns and other equipment to protect themselves from the mountain bears and lions.

There was plain grassy land on the mountains at several regions, where a few shepherds grazed their sheep and cattle on the alpages and lived on the mountains. Jacob and his companions talked to the shepherds, to get a better idea about the route and path they needed to take, to reach the mid of timberline on the north face. As there was no specified road or trail, they had to pass through the rough, craggy terrain to reach the timberline. They had their rucksacks with all the equipment needed and some food and water. As they travelled, they felt cheerful and enthusiastic because the mission had begun in a true sense.

Gilbert was ahead of them, and he introduced

several native trees to all, especially, varieties of spruce and pines. He also introduced a few native mountain animals and birds. He swaggered that he knew the mountain better, and all the others followed him towards the mid of timberline.

'Do you know something?' said Gilbert. 'I already knew about Georgina's spirit! My grandfather used to tell me stories about this thief, Jungle Jett, and a little about his wife, Georgina when I was a kid. The wife was supposed to be a brilliant woman though she is not very famous among the villagers. There have always been rumours among the village people that her spirit does exist on Mount Jett, guarding the treasure, but I never believed it because I thought it was all a made-up story. Now I think I better believe it so that we can get success in the chase,' he said trotting on his horse as he addressed the others following him.

'Oh, really!' said Jacob, who was behind him, very next to Gilbert. 'You cannot force yourself to believe in it, Gilbert. You need to concentrate, focus and meditate to connect with the belief that Georgina's spirit exists and that could make our errand much easier, and that's what Glinda expects from us.'

'My grandfather always advised my father and me never to try chasing the treasure because he did not want us to risk our lives,' said Gilbert. 'He said that Georgina's demon was very evil and passionate about the hidden wealth. These older people are so naive and easily believe in such baloney. But look, now I am here with you guys, against my grandpa's advice and all odds, trying to chase the treasure all over again,' he said sardonically with hope against hope.

He continued, 'A few youths who tried privately and the people hired by the government who tried finding this treasure have been dead and lost. The village people down the mountain, believe that it was Georgina's monster who killed them. But don't you think it seems a little absurd! Maybe all those adventurous men died due to the wilderness and difficulty in mountaineering and the enigmatic glaciers. I don't give credence to this tittle-tattle. A few have tried reaching the summit, thinking that the treasure could be hidden somewhere there but died even before they could reach the peak. Some did reach the peak, I guess, but nobody knows what happened to them because they never came back. By the way, Jacob and Peter, you guys are highly technical, of course, that's what I assume. So, how can you believe in the theory of ghosts and spirits? How could you be superstitious?' challenged Gilbert.

'Basically, I do not believe in the presence of ghosts,' said Jacob and continued analyzing the matter. 'Moreover, the term 'ghosts' feels like a very evil and negative word. 'Spirit or soul' of the dead, sounds more positive and non-evil. Wandering spirits or souls may be evil or good depending on the situation, just like humans. Somehow, after coming here and meeting up with Glinda, I think, what she said makes sense. So yeah, from a certain angle, I have started to believe I guess, though not in any other ghost, but Georgina's spirit,... YES! Georgina's story with her husband Jungle Jett seems so lasting and still functioning. It doesn't seem like it happened more than a century ago. It feels like their life still exists because the couple led such an eventful and challenging life. We know for sure that Jungle Jett died and was buried with last rites by Georgina. We don't know what happened to Georgina after that. So, especially Georgina appears extant to me, whatever form she may be in, at the moment, as she was a strong and passionate woman. If we regard the existence of her spirit as real and request her with solemn devotion to help us, her soul might appreciate us and eventually allow us to achieve our goal,' said Jacob with optimism.

'I have one big doubt,' said Gilbert. 'Even with all these disasters and deaths that happened with the people who tried chasing the treasure on Mount Jett, the old witch Glinda wouldn't budge. She wouldn't enlighten anybody with her secret information, the particulars about the caves and the treasure. I wonder how she got stirred this time.

Jacob and Peter, what was that she saw in you two, that made her flexible and ready to help?' asked Gilbert.

'That part is a mystery even to us, and Glinda wouldn't explain it,' said Peter.

When they almost reached the timberline, it was mid-noon. They inspected the surroundings to study the landscape. Above the tree line, the mountain was all bleak and rocky. Gilbert pointed at the volcanoes, that were seen far away from about seven to eight miles. Adrian told them that one of the volcanoes out there, called 'Mount Pirate', was active, while the other volcanoes remained dormant for hundreds of years. Using their binocular, they saw a faint cloud of grey gas emerging from the top of Mount Pirate. Gilbert said there had been a few mild earthquakes in the villages and the mountains, in the recent past and that the villagers and townsmen had to evacuate just before one eruption that happened ten years back at Mount Pirate. They all looked at the volcanoes, surprised.

After reaching the probable location, they dismounted and sat on the rocks to rest in the shades of the topmost trees. They ate a light meal, drank energy drinks and relaxed for a while. Jacob did a thorough search in the area for the clue that Glinda had given to locate where exactly to begin the excavation for the idol. There, he found a tiny cross, facing north, carved on a huge rocky boulder. The cross was almost invisible if one wasn't watchful. His heart filled with warmth and hope. He instructed the men to start digging the earth below the cross.

They started to dig the probable location. Glinda had said, Buddha idol and Jungle Jett's body were buried approximately at a depth of 10 feet under the surface which was more than the usual for a burial. Jacob had a hi-end metal detector which could detect at least 5 feet deep. So they just kept digging and used the metal detector on and off. It was such a laborious job, but as they were six of them, full of enthusiasm, they managed to dig faster. The six men had dug 8 feet wide and 10 feet deep into the ground by dusk. The rockiness was less there, which made it easier to dig. The metal detector detected few metals on and off, but they turned out to be some artefacts, coins, and metal plates that were not much valuable.

They managed to dig 12 feet deep. Still, they did not find anything worthy, which was quite discouraging. Brayan felt restless and cursed the old witch. 'Looks like, that crazy woman has gambled with us. I think she has fooled us. Darn it!' he said with bitterness.

'Take it easy, Brayan,' said Peter. 'I am sure she wouldn't gamble with us. If Glinda wanted to fool people like us, she would have kept doing that to all people who tried to get help from her instead of denying them the information. She would have set a budget for the information she gave. She hasn't done anything of that sort. Maybe, the idol is somewhere nearby, around this place itself. Maybe the probable place we dug was slightly away from the actual location. Maybe the actual location is somewhere nether to the present one. Trust and patience are all we need at the moment, to boost our confidence level. If we do our job with frustration, we would be deprived of all our energy to pursue the chase. So it is important to keep relevant from the beginning until the end of the mission. We need to maintain the thrill of chasing Mount Jett, against all odds,' he tried to perk Brayan up with some inspiration.

'I guess you are right. We'll rest a bit and then start digging after midnight, a little lower than this spot,' suggested Jacob. Everybody was tired and decided to rest at the timberline for the night. Though it was quite cold at that height, they were comfortable because they'd come well prepared with their tents and blankets. They were famished, and as they started to have dinner, Jacob initiated a conversation with Gilbert.

'Gilbert, what do you do for a living?' Jacob asked.

'I don't do anything in particular. My father has a business, and most of the times I help him with it like an apprentice, which I am not happy about. I'm my parents' only son, and there is no much pressure on me regarding my work for a living. They are happy enough to look after me as long as they are alive and healthy,' said Gilbert.

How disgusting could that be, being dependent on parents even at this age! Maybe the village kids of this region are brought up like that, thought Peter.

Gilbert continued, 'So, not having a particular job of my own, I'm after the treasure to make some king's ransom for myself, to show my worth to my parents. I've been waiting for a windfall all along,' said Gilbert, feeling impatient.

Jacob looked at him with suspicion. 'Gilbert, what kind of a business is your father into?' he asked.

'My father runs a motel, and I do silly chores for him in that stupid business of his. I hate the boring routine of my life, though,' said Gilbert.

'Ok, are you married?' Jacob asked.

'Nope,' said Gilbert. Jacob noticed Gilbert's expression changing into a grimace. 'But, I do have a girlfriend,' he said somberly, as if, having a girlfriend was a curse.

'Why do you grimace? Are you not happy to be having a girlfriend?' Asked Jacob.

'I don't know. The worst part is, my girlfriend

is missing from one week,' he said, and Jacob was alarmed.

Peter was curious and asked Gilbert, 'What do you mean....she is missing? Did she run away with another guy? Or did anybody kidnap her?'

'No, she could never dare to run away with another guy!' said Gilbert. 'She is a timid little creature. If she has run away with another guy, I will kill her when I find her back. But, no such scenario at the moment, hopefully,' he said.

'Which village are you from and what is your girlfriend's name?' Asked Jacob with great curiosity, expecting the inevitable.

'How does that matter to you? It's none of your business,' said Gilbert sternly. 'Anyway, what's my loss in answering your question? I'm from the village Figlington, and my girlfriend's name is Rose,' said Gilbert.

Jacob kind of sighed with relief and thought, *Olivia is from Figlington too but thank goodness she is not Gilbert's girlfriend; instead, his girlfriend is someone else by name, Rose.*

'I mean, Rose is her nickname, but her real name is Olivia,' said Gilbert immediately and Jacob's heart missed a beat. Jacob took some time to pull himself together before he could think further. *Oh, my Goodness! Olivia never once uttered her ex-boyfriend's name! And I never cared to ask!* He felt angry on Gilbert for having been rude to Olivia and for having ill-treated her before. He also felt good because, if Gilbert hadn't ill-treated Olivia, she wouldn't have escaped from Gilbert and met Jacob.

This is going to be a risky affair, though! It's good that I talked to Gilbert about his personal life. What a coincidence! Now that I know Gilbert is Olivia's ex, I need to be cautious and never let Gilbert or anyone know that Olivia is staying with me. I must alert Olivia and tell her to be extremely careful and not be seen by anyone. Jacob decided.

They started digging near the last spot after some time, but a little lower. They had the head torches that aided them in their errand. After digging a few inches, they found a few artefacts which were not of much importance to them. By dawn, they had managed to dig 12 feet deeper the second time, but to no avail. Ultimately their whole effort to find the Buddha idol had gone waste. They were tired and upset, but they knew that chasing a treasure was not a child's play.

Jacob and Peter tried their best to cheer the others up. Jacob said he would meet Glinda again the next day to find a solution. He said maybe the idol was also hidden somewhere in the caves along with the brass chest and advised them not to lose hopes. They all slumped tired on the ground and went off to sleep in their sleeping bags till next noon.

This time, Jacob was not worried that Olivia would be waiting for him restlessly because he had given her prior intimation about the day's errand. When he'd come to know that, Gilbert himself was her evil ex-boyfriend, he had been a little shaken, but had recovered soon enough, thinking, it was all a coincidence and destiny, and whatever was going to happen next, would happen for the best. Jacob decided to keep Olivia behind the screen, out of anyone's sight, just like how Jungle Jett had kept Georgina from the outside world. He was determined to let her stay with him, a core secret, like the treasure itself, and it was his duty to guard this precious treasure of love.

Brayan had seen Jacob's cabin, and so Jacob thought he needed to be careful henceforth. He was not worried about Peter. Jacob decided to see to it that, forthwith, Brayan never brought Gilbert anywhere near his cabin. Alternatively, he tried to analyze whether he could change his cabin's location. But, that was out of the question at the moment, with a busy schedule and things moving at a faster pace. He decided that Olivia was destined to belong to him and only him. *What if I could not find Buddha idol, I have found the precious treasure of love in Olivia. She loves me, and I love her, and that makes our lives perfect and complete.* Thinking so, he felt solace and fell into a deep sleep.

CHAPTER 9

~~~~~ 🙂 ~~~~~

That evening, Jacob returned to his cabin before sundown, longing to see Olivia at the earliest. After conversing with Gilbert, his emotions towards Olivia had grown stronger. This time his feelings were intense and feverish, longing for her touch and comfort. As he dismounted from his horse at the cabin, Olivia came running and hugged him. Olivia looked beautiful and prettier than ever. She looked like a goddess of love and as pure as the driven snow.

'I missed you, Jacob,' she murmured, lifting her heels and kissing him on his cheek. After a hectic and disappointing expedition, Jacob felt greatly comforted in her warm, tender hug.

'I missed you badly too,' he said, cupping her face with his palms, returning her kiss.

The two of them went inside the cabin holding each other's backs. As they sat on the porch watching the sunset and sipping coffee, Jacob narrated to her, the previous day's events, even though she did not ask any questions regarding it. He felt surprised that he was confiding in her without his knowledge and felt good about the same. He thought she deserved to know everything that was happening with him and his adventure because now she had become a significant part of his routine on the lonely mountain.

'Jacob, you had strictly told me not to ask any questions about your mission,' said Olivia. 'So I'm not asking you anything because I am confused about what to ask and what not to ask,' she confessed.

'No worries, Olivia,' said Jacob. 'You can ask me anything you want to know. I've started to confide in you, which shows I have started to like you and trust you. I feel you deserve to know everything about me and my mission,' he said, looking tenderly at her, studying her strands of loose hair that floated on her face in response to the cool breeze.

'Thank you, Jacob,' said Olivia happily. 'I'm happy and feel honoured by this statement of yours,' she said, kissing him again on his cheeks. He moved the strands of her hair from her face and tucked them behind her ears with his fingers.

'Did you encounter the thudding and hammering sounds yesterday night as well?' he asked her with concern.

'Jacob, yesterday night I couldn't sleep till midnight because I was alone and anxious. But after midnight I fell fast asleep, and I guess, I missed hearing the weird sounds even if they were there. I am not sure,' she said. 'These days, I think I've gotten used to these strange sounds because I don't hear them anymore, I guess. But two days back I heard them, while you were sleeping on the couch and I noticed that the hidden green bag in the backyard was missing as well. When the sounds stopped, I checked again in the backyard, and the green bag was safely back there in its usual place. So I'm not sure what is happening, and I am worried that I might be hallucinating,' she said in a worried tone.

'That's ok, never mind. You are not hallucinating. The sounds truly exist, and I know where they come from. I will enlighten you with the same when the time is right,' he said, appeasing her.

'Really? I was worried that someone was stalking you intending to harm you. That means, is it any of your associates who are using your tools from the green bag and working somewhere nearby on your project?' she asked him curiously.

'I said I'll let you know about it soon enough. You don't have to break your head over that matter at the moment. It's nothing to be worried about. Trust me. I can ensure you again that we are quite safe here,' he said. Olivia was relieved and promised him that she would never worry about the queer sounds again.

'Olivia,' Jacob said, looking deeply into her sparkling blue eyes. 'I was very much worried about the fact that you were all alone in the cabin yesterday. By the way, I need to ask you about something very important.' She looked curiously at him. 'What is your ex-boyfriend's name?' he asked.

'Oh, come on, Jacob. I'm trying to forget everything and anything about my ex-boyfriend. I don't want even to utter his name. Why do you want to know what his name is? He is my past, and I don't care about him anymore,' she said with a determined tone, at the same time, feeling edgy.

'Of course, it's important that I should know his name from you,' Jacob said.

'Ok, he's Gilbert, the crooked,' she said full of disgust.

Jacob took a deep breath to calm his mind a bit. *What a coincidence that Gilbert is accompanying us in this treasure hunt!* Thought Jacob and laughed to himself sardonically.

'Why are you smiling, Jacob? What's so funny about his name?' she asked, smiling.

'Olivia, we need to be truly careful. This ex-boyfriend of yours is on the mountains,' he said, trying to study her expressions.

'WHAT?! Do you think he is on the mountain, searching for me?' she asked, panicked.

'Not like that. Gilbert is searching, not for you, but for the hidden treasure,' he said.

'Oh, really?! That son of a bitch! Fortunately, he

is not searching for me, which means I'm safe. How do you know that he is after the treasure? He has ventured to chase the treasure many times, every time in vain,' she said.

'Ok, fortunately, he is not searching for you. But unfortunately, he is assisting me on the hunt for treasure right on this mountain,' Jacob said, while she looked at him bewildered and shocked. 'It's all a coincidence that I got in touch with him on business, without knowing he is the one behind your pathetic old love story.... sorry to say that way,' Jacob confessed. 'It was Brayan who introduced Gilbert to us,' he said, while she looked restless.

'Jacob, do you think I am safe here staying with you? Are you going to send me away from your cabin and yourself? I truly do not want to bring you any trouble. If you want me to quit, I will. I'll do whatever you say,' she said with a sad face looking down at the ground.

'Olivia, I do not want to send you away from me. I want you to stay with me as much as you want to stay with me. I love your company, but....'

'But what, Jacob?' she looked solicitous.

'But you need to be extra cautious henceforth. I do not want any of my associates seeing you by any chance,' he advised.

She looked happy and hugged him tightly and said, 'Sure, Jacob, I'll stay inside the cabin and never come out of it, if that's what you mean. I can do anything, as long as you let me stay here. I feel safe with you,' she agreed.

'I do not want you to lock yourself up in the cabin. You can freely walk about but just be extremely careful,' he said.

'Sure, Jacob. But I have one doubt. You said that Roark's spies are supervising the whole mission. What if they come to know that I am staying here with you? Do you think they might report about me to Roark and bring you trouble?' she asked.

'I guess not. Your staying with me will not disrupt the mission in any way, as long as you remain to yourself and not get involved in anything mischievous. So why would the spies care or why would Roark care about your stay here? You are staying here with me because you just need shelter, a roof above your head and I want you to stay with me too. You are in no way concerned with the mission and thus harmless. Roark is protective of his truthful employees. I know I am truthful to him. He wouldn't mind your stay with me I guess, as long as I remain true to him, and as long as you mind your own business without snooping around, that's all,' he said caressing her cheeks and enjoying the touch and feel of her rosy translucent faultless cheeks.

'Rose, I think I have started to like you a lot,' he

said, and the two of them laughed at the way he addressed her as Rose.

~ ~ ~ ~

The next day, Jacob and Peter met the old witch, Glinda. They had lots to confide in her about their hopelessly failed attempt to retrieve Buddha idol. They wanted to know what could be the reason for the failure, even though they had given their best.

Glinda thought for a while and said, 'Don't you worry, Jacob. I'm here to help you. This whole thing is very complicated and not a kid's play. I'd told you that, finding Buddha idol could be associated with some obstacles. It needs a lot of patience and determination to unearth the treasure of this calibre. We need to go about it methodically. So, I undoubtedly feel that it needs a spiritual solution. I can sense that, with the time approaching for the mountain to reveal, Georgina's spirit has become more powerful than ever.' Glinda looked quite stable with her health and very eager to help Jacob and Peter.

'So, do you think Georgina's spirit is going to pose a stronger hurdle in our expedition?' asked Peter worried.

Glinda gestured him to calm down, did some tarot reading, and waved her wand in the air and thought deeply for a few minutes. Finally, she said with a firm voice. 'We need to perform a ritual for the exorcism of Georgina's spirit.' Jacob was alarmed to hear that. 'Georgina's spirit, guarding the treasure, is the biggest obstacle in your venture. We need to perform the ritual to communicate with her soul and convince her that, this is the right time and you are the right person. You can never get your hands on the treasure unless Georgina decides to leave it all to you. We must convince her that we all love her; you love her,' she said to Jacob confidently. 'By performing this ritual, Georgina's soul can be rendered calm and allowed to rest in peace. Now guarantee me that you believe in the existence of her spirit,' she said to Jacob.

'Of course, I swear, I believe and trust in Georgina's spirit wholeheartedly. I have strong faith that she is there in the mountains with all her passion, guarding the treasure. I literally can visualize her being on guard of the hidden treasure,' Jacob said with great confidence. Glinda was glad and felt convinced.

'So, first, we need to fix a time and venue for the ritual. Tomorrow is a new moon day with the darkest of the nights. On this night of the month, her spirit will be more alert, passionate, vulnerable and easier to communicate with. So I would like to perform the ritual tomorrow at midnight, by the bank of White River on Mount Jett. It would help if you made arrangements to take me there to the allotted spot to perform the ritual. I will give you a list of things needed for the ritual, which you need to arrange at the venue before my arrival,' instructed Glinda. Jacob and Peter looked at her, stunned with wide eyes and gave their approval. At this moment, they were in accord with whatever Glinda suggested; they had to be; there was no other go; she was their only guiding star.

'You look panicked,' Glinda said to Jacob and Peter. 'There's nothing to worry about when I'm around to help you out. I'll take care to see that I conduct the ritual in a perfectly safe way,' she assured.

'Is this ritual safe to all of us? What if Georgina's spirit hurts someone?' asked Peter.

'Don't you worry. I know that Georgina's spirit is a good one- wouldn't harm anyone unless anyone means to harm her. If we wish good for her and convince her that the treasure hunt is for a good cause, then she'll undoubtedly get evicted from the mountain, wishing us good, leaving all the wealth to you. We need to perform the procedure with great love and respect for her soul, instead of treating her like someone evil.' Glinda advised.

Jacob and Peter felt solace with her assurance. 'There's one condition from my side, though,' said Glinda. 'Please don't let Brayan and Gilbert participate in the ritual. I want them far away from the venue because they might get hurt in the process as they seem unfaithful,' she cautioned. 'Georgina wouldn't like unfaithful people.'

'I'll inform Brayan and Gilbert to keep away during the ritual,' assured Jacob.

'And one more thing is mandatory. We need a lamb that would be offered and sacrificed during the ritual,' she instructed. The duo promised to arrange everything.

Jacob and Peter felt nervous about the whole thing, but they were in no stage to doubt the spirit and Glinda's visions. That would offend the whole spiritual thing attached with the treasure, and they might end up being disappointed. They had to believe in and trust the spirit and the ritual, to make it a success. Though scientifically, all this looked weird; emotionally and spiritually, it seemed like a perfect thing to do. It would provide them with confidence and enthusiasm to chase further. It would act as a placebo in their venture. Thus they decided not to disregard this belief. *If the ritual could help us in any possible way, then there is no harm in going with it, as it would provide a positive green signal for the expedition,* thought Jacob.

Glinda looked happy, lively and showed improvement in her health condition. She gave them the list of things to be arranged for the ritual and explained the ritual's brief procedure. She said that, apart from a lamb's sacrifice, the rest of the ceremony would be a simple prayer and communication process with the powerful cosmic elements and thus, the spirit.

~ ~ ~ ~

When Jacob returned to the cabin and conveyed all the news to Olivia, Olivia was thrilled and asked eagerly, 'Jacob, I would love to participate in the ritual too. Can I come with you?'. She asked this, though she was aware that she needed to be extremely careful and in the hideout at the moment. She just couldn't resist asking Jacob because she thought it would be a spiritual experience, in fact, an experience of a lifetime. She hoped that there could be some other alternate way for her to attend the ritual without being noticed or seen. She had never heard or seen anything like it before, so was excited by the mere thought of communicating with a spirit.

'Of course not. How can you even think of being seen with me in this scenario?' said Jacob, dismissing her idea. She felt sombre and pleaded him to find a way because she did not want to miss this lifetime opportunity.

'Jacob, where there is a will, there is a way. You sure can let me participate in the ritual, can't you?' she supplicated hopefully. He looked at her face and saw that she was desperate.

'Ok,' he said, 'but on one condition.'

'Okay sure, by any condition whatsoever,... please... please ....please!' she begged again.

'Fine, I'll try and find a way for you to participate but not with me,' he said, and she agreed. Anyway, he thought it was ok if she attended the ritual because Gilbert would not be there, as per Glinda's instructions.

The next day was another momentous day. Jacob and his colleagues were busy making arrangements for the ritual. They had fixed a venue by the White River bank on the east face of Mount Jett as Glinda had said, the brass chest with the treasure was hidden in the secret caves whose entrance was on the east face of Mount Jett. The venue was kind of a circular plain sandy, grassy and verdant terrain by the river, desolate and far away from the human habitation. The area was embosomed by the densely grown spruce and pine trees and thus secluded from the mountain's surrounding part. The venue was perfect for the clandestine ritual of the dark.

Jacob suggested Brayan and Gilbert not to participate in the ritual. He explained that it was in their interest; they might get hurt if they tried to come anywhere near the venue. Though Gilbert and Brayan hopped madly with this instruction, they had to agree because it was a question of their life and death. Still, they were cross with Glinda because they thought she was rude and mean towards them.

The most awaited night approached. Richard and Sarah brought Glinda to the ritual venue by the White River bank, after dusk. Jacob and Olivia dismounted from Thunder a little distance away from the ritual ground. Olivia was wearing a long greyish black cloak and a mask that Jacob had given her for the purpose. There was no chance of anyone recognizing her at the ceremony with the cloak and the mask. They walked for a short distance to reach the venue through the darkness of the jungle, though Olivia walked a little distance behind Jacob. She was very excited about the whole thing. Before Jacob went to meet Glinda and the others, he suggested Olivia to wait behind a tree in anticipation of the right moment, to, later on, join in with the others, without anyone's knowledge. Still, he was worried that Olivia could get hurt during the ritual and decided to safeguard her.

Glinda was glad to see Jacob and the others. The night was star-spangled but almost pitch dark because the moon was absent and the surrounding jungle was dense. Peter had brought a perfect lamb and had tied it to a nearby tree.

Olivia was surprised to see that, apart from the people concerned with the project, there were several other people, at least a dozen of them, wearing cloaks and masks- similar to the ones she was wearing. *This is going to be exciting,* thought Olivia. She looked around to scrutinize if Gilbert was about, but was relieved not seeing him anywhere. She moved gently in the dark and joined the people with the cloaks and masks. Now she was one among them though she could not discern, whether they were men or women...., *maybe both;* she assumed.

To her amazement, the people in cloaks did not appear normal and oriented. They swayed with their eyes in the clouds. They seemed like they had no presence of mind. Olivia felt thrilled. While the others had their eyes in the clouds, she was on the cloud nine with excitement. *Olivia, don't be kiddish*! She warned herself. *It's not a joke. If something goes wrong, it might even cost your life,* she thought and tried to come down on her foot, then became serious with a keen interest in observing the ritual.

Peter looked suspiciously at the people with the cloaks, trying to analyze who all those people were; with so many strangers around, how could the ceremony be a secret shady affair. Jacob came to his aid and cleared his doubts.

'Peter, all these people are Glinda's followers, and they also include her grandson Richard and his wife Sarah and many other men and women. Glinda has assured me these people are harmless because they are in a trance, a state of stupor;

hypnotised, or drugged. They don't even know that they are here at the moment. But being in a trance and under a spell, they are the right people to attract the cosmic elements, making it easier to communicate with the spirit. They can communicate with the cosmos, better than the oriented people because, at the moment, their wits are not in this world. They are lost in a brown study, and their minds have merged with the universe. They can grasp, pick, and attract the virtual world's unknown cosmic elements, better than normal and alert humans.' Peter was amazed to know about this aspect.

Glinda stood at the centre of the ground, looking fit as a fiddle, even though she was very old. It seemed like she had almost recovered from her infirmity and was bursting with child-like grace and enthusiasm. She instructed the others to make a big circle around her, and all obeyed.

An unlit candle was given to each one of them. Glinda lit a candle herself, said some prayers and blessed the candle in her hand. She gave it to Jacob and instructed him to light all the candles in the followers' hands. He did as instructed. When all the candles were lit, Olivia saw the glowing candle in her hand and felt delighted. She was invigorated seeing the orange, sweet-smelling, flickering flame in her hand. She quivered when a drop of hot molten wax dropped on her bare hand. All of them raised the blessed candles towards the summit, as they continued to sway and mumble some unknown incantations. Olivia did the same, prayed passionately and truthfully from the bottom of her heart, wishing for the ritual and the mission to become successful.

All their tools and equipment for the treasure hunt were also displayed in the centre. It was part of the ritual, with the intension of rendering the equipment, more powerful, to detect and unearth the treasure. Glinda started to say her prayers and the people kept swaying sideways, to and fro. The mid-summer night was quite sultry, and they were all sweating. After praying for half an hour, Glinda instructed the people to revolve and rotate. All of them started to move in a circle still swaying, while some of them even began to dance to the music of Glinda's prayers. They all joined in her incantations. The whole thing seemed spooky and scary; still, thrilling. Suddenly, Glinda stopped her prayers and instructed Richard to get squeaky clean lamb bursting with health and instructed him to offer it to the spirit.

The people in the cloaks were soon invigorated and started to sway and dance briskly in the circle, making weird noises, jumping and swirling. Olivia had a tough time keeping in pace with them. With the fear of being recognized, she also jumped and danced with them, letting herself go. At some point during the night, she felt like she was in a trance herself, as she had devotedly participated in the ritual.

Richard offered the sacrifice by killing the lamb. He cut its throat, collected its blood in a trough and sprinkled it into the river and the surrounding areas at the venue. They all prayed to the mountain to reveal itself. This part of the ritual was hair-raising and intimidating to Olivia, though she had indulged herself with complete steadfastness in the practice of the darkness.

Glinda waved her divining rod at the skies and focused on nature and the universe. She instructed Richard to provide a blessed drink to all those who had participated, including herself. Everybody consumed the potion that was offered by Richard. After they all finished the drink, everything changed. All of them went into a deeper trance and felt high, dancing and trying to reach the elements in the universe, calling out for Georgina's spirit to show herself.

Suddenly, a brisk wind started to blow, and the atmosphere became cold and nippy. It looked like a thunderstorm was on its way. Glinda announced that Georgina's spirit was trying to communicate with them in this manner and advised everyone to be alert and careful. The candles went out in the forcefully blowing wind, and an ebony blackness surrounded them all, from everywhere. The people in cloaks held on to each other's backs and danced vigorously around Glinda as if they were now in contact with the spirit, welcoming it to be a part of them, to be one among them. The sprightliness of the people's buzz and the crispness of the brisk wind rose to a crescendo, and Olivia felt like she was flying high up in the air.

Olivia shuddered with all the unexpected bustling around her and the weather transformation, more of a pulse severe storm, as it started to rain in torrents, with lightning, thunder and spanking breeze. Her head started to ache badly, and she was about to blackout when Jacob instantly supported her. While Olivia recovered, she realized Jacob was beside her all that while, which she'd failed to notice, due to her utter solitary mood at the time. Now she felt safe again. It rained stair rods for at least half an hour, while the people in cloaks all soaked to their skins, kept dancing, swaying, praying and jumping. Glinda started to shout out her prayers loudly and gestured everyone to look up at the summit of Mount Jett. Soon the rain stopped; the breeze calmed; there appeared a sharp white light on top of the mountain like a star, at the base of the summit on the east face of Mount Jett, illuminating the venue with its intense blaze.

Everyone was enthralled to see the star of Georgina's spirit on top of the mountain and exclaimed in awe, dazzled by its glare. That was the climax of the ritual. Glinda pointed with her divining rod, at the white light on the summit and announced that it was Georgina's spirit out there, with them. Everyone was entranced; their hearts thumping heavily. Olivia was too excited to see how Georgina's spirit showed itself high up on Mount Jett, at the base of its summit. Glinda proceeded with her incantations and put in all her skills into convincing Georgina's spirit that it was time for her to stop guarding the treasure, quit the mountain and rest in peace forever.

Soon enough, the faint light disappeared, the thunderstorm alleviated and the whole dark jungle appeared to have calmed down. Glinda thanked everyone for their support and devotion. The lamb was soon slain, roasted, shared and consumed by each one of them, along with the holy wine supplied. Everyone enjoyed the midnight meal and fell on to the ground, exhausted. They blacked out after a queer event which ended just before daybreak.

Glinda sat meditating till dawn. At sunrise, she woke Jacob up. The rest of the followers were still sleeping. She asked Jacob to follow her. He observed that Glinda looked like a treasure of infinite power in the fresh hours of dayspring.

He was amazed to see that Glinda was walking gracefully with the energy of a child. She pointed towards the base of the summit on the east face and said to Jacob. 'The treasure is all yours now. The only thing you've got to do is to dig for the caves' entrance on the east face to unveil the treasure. You will undoubtedly find the brass chest.'

She also explained to him the landmark where exactly he was to start digging the ice for the hidden caves. He was happy and thrilled. She also confirmed that he would undoubtedly find the Buddha idol, though she did not know how or where. She confirmed that Georgina's spirit had ultimately evicted the mountain and that he was free to explore without any obstacles. The ritual, Glinda's assurance and the landmarks explained to him by her, gave Jacob a leap of faith for their mission's success.

Glinda soon produced an envelope from her side pocket and gave it to Jacob. 'Jacob, you can open this envelope, only after you find the treasure. Till then keep it safe,' she instructed. She also whispered some queer things in his ears. Jacob was delighted and thanked Glinda for everything. He was dazed by the previous night's fantastic experience and badly needed to rest. He woke Olivia up, and they returned to the cabin before the others were up. Glinda went back to her shack with Richard and Sarah, feeling great. Peter and Glinda's followers went back to their respective abodes, as and when they got up, not remembering what had happened all night through, though they knew it was something to do with the old witch, Glinda and her ritual.

CHAPTER 10

'Jacob, it was such a wonderful experience,' said Olivia, preparing sandwiches for lunch, 'an experience of a lifetime, at least for me. Even though I was not drugged or hypnotized, I felt completely entranced. The ritual venue and its ambience out there was ecstatic, so crazy and full of fantasy. I experienced something so improbable even in my dreams. But the offering of the lamb to Georgina's spirit was kind of spooky.' Olivia was still in the hangover of the eventful ritual, obsessed after her confrontation with all the strange followers and their incantations. The glaring light of Georgina's spirit seen high up on the summit had bewitched her. It was a celestial sight from the other world.

'True,' said Jacob, who was relaxing on the couch with a beer bottle in his hand. 'It was one hell of an experience. I was worried that you would get hurt. You sure did enjoy quite a lot, didn't you?' he said, smiling and nictitating at her.

'I know,' she said gladly. 'I never knew you were right there beside me, the whole time during the ritual. I thought I had joined the people in cloaks and masks, without anybody's knowledge, even without yours,' she laughed, 'and by the way, what was that potion Glinda offered everyone to drink?' she asked curiously.

'I don't know what exactly it was because it might have been her secret energy drink,' he said chuckling.

'But you know, what?' said Olivia, 'after consuming the potion, I started to feel euphoric and light as cotton; I wasn't even aware of what was happening around me until you held me, saving me from collapsing. Only then did I realize that you were by my side. Did you consume the potion as well, Jacob?' she asked, curiously because it seemed to her that Jacob had been well under control.

'Of course, I consumed the potion, and I had to. It was part of Glinda's ritual, and I wouldn't let her down by any means. Glinda was there to help us, and it was my duty to follow her every instruction. But maybe, I was not as sensitive as you, to the effects of the drink. I was quite alert and stable during the whole process. But for you, I guess you were completely exhausted, after all the swirling, jumping and dancing, that made you lose balance,' he said.

'Wow, did you see the blazing light, the star of Georgina's spirit that appeared along with a thunderstorm and how it later disappeared and made the whole jungle calm and black? At that juncture, the experience was phenomenal and spellbinding; felt like a different world altogether. Do you think the light that appeared on the summit could be a real spirit or one of Glinda's magic?' she asked curiously.

'Honestly, Olivia, I do not want to interpret what happened during the ritual. Glinda needed me to believe in the spirit, and I just obeyed her with all my heart. I trust and still believe that everything has been right, that's all, and do not want to analyze anything. But undoubtedly, Gods willing, the whole event has given me a lot of hopes and has boosted my confidence level. That is the most crucial thing needed to pursue the treasure with optimism, I reckon. Why should it matter whether it was magic or a reality? We all at one point of time need to believe that there is a virtual world beyond our senses, and at times, there is a possibility that we might get to communicate with our counterparts. Who knows for sure, what is real or what is a myth? Moreover, Glinda didn't charge me a dime for the ritual except for the arrangements. That indicates she is more than genuine and truly wants to help me.

We, humans, are just dust particles belonging to the universe. Our powers are limited too, and we cannot interpret everything scientifically. Glinda is the oldest soul, and on top of that, she is a witch. Undoubtedly, I believe that she has special powers inculcated through her practices and experiences over the past century. So I believe she is genuine and truly wants to help me. Let's wait and see what happens next. If we find the treasure, my faith towards her powers will be boosted. Even if I do not find the treasure, I won't consider it her fault; instead, I would accept it as my destiny or fate, due to some other unexpected hindering elements operating in the universe beyond our control. But no matter what, I have come to trust in Glinda,' he justified.

Olivia was amazed by his explanation. 'Wow, Jacob, you are such a positive and sanguine person. People like you are bound to get success. I appreciate your forbearance and will-power,' she said, passing over his lunch plate.

'Do you know something?' he asked her as if he would tell her some secret. 'Early today morning at daybreak, Glinda led me on foot, to a particular place, away from everyone. There she pointed at the base of the summit and explained the location, where we could start digging for the hidden caves' entrance. The amazing part is that Glinda walked youthfully this morning, even though she has been old and ill. That explains her vivacity and zeal that she had been so eagerly waiting all her life, for the right person to reveal the mountain. She looked very happy and relieved this morning, after conveying me the details about the location. She also said a few prayers, placed her palm on my head and blessed me to imbibe all the confidence and grace. After that, I felt truly energized. Honestly, she is someone proficient in her job. She knows what she is doing. Whether I find the treasure or not, I would be grateful to her for all the help she is offering me,' he said with deep emotions.

Jacob did not mention the envelope that Glinda had given him and what Glinda had whispered into his ears. He decided it wasn't necessary at the moment.

Jacob and Olivia rested in the afternoon and watched the sunset in the evening. Life seemed so beautiful to Olivia in Jacob's company, with all the pleasant unexpected and exciting things that were happenings at the moment in her life.

'Jacob, I feel so blessed at the moment,' she said. 'I always want to be with you till my last breath,' she said, hoping her wish would come true. She imagined that the orange sun sinking behind the mountains miles away blessed her for her dream to come true. The cool breeze kissing her face and tweeting of the birds returning to their nests were the witnesses for the blessing.

~ ~ ~ ~

That night, Olivia woke up again with a start, hearing the thudding and hammering sounds. She was startled. Olivia doubted if anyone apart from Jacob and his associates had begun digging for the treasure, long back. She tried concentrating and felt agitated when she couldn't make out anything.

This mountain is so mysterious, can't even discern where the sounds are coming from. I cannot thole with this puzzle anymore. What if somebody else finds the treasure before Jacob? But she knew that it was impossible because she trusted Glinda, her visions and her successful ritual, blessing Jacob. Even though Jacob had assured her that he knew about the sounds and that he would enlighten her with the same when the time was right, she was in an adventurous mood. She decided to discover the source of the freakish sounds that night, though she knew Jacob would disapprove of her playing a sticky beak.

She wrapped herself with the blanket and came to the living room with hope against hope. As usual, Jacob was sleeping tight, as seen in the faint shimmering moonlight. She emerged from the cabin, scanned the surroundings, advanced to the cabin's backyard, and found that the green bag of tools was missing again. *Good God! This is too much. Jacob said it was his bag; he is sleeping tight on the couch, and now the bag is missing again. What the hell is happening out here?* She felt like she was feeling dizzy with her clumsy thoughts.

This time, she decided, she was going to wake Jacob up. Though she felt guilty about disturbing him, she put her guilt at bay and shook Jacob tenderly. 'Jacob, wake up, I need your help. I hear the weird sounds again. I need to know what's happening out here.'

Jacob did not stir a bit. She shook him again with a little extra force, and a long pillow fell on to the ground from the couch. Olivia was shocked to know that it was the pillow that she was shaking and trying to wake, thinking it was Jacob sleeping tight. She was stunned to learn that Jacob was not on his couch; instead, it was just a long pillow that she had thought was Jacob. *So, all these days, I was fooled into believing that Jacob was sleeping on the couch, and someone else was digging.* Now, it was clear that Jacob himself had been digging somewhere with his tools from the big green leather bag.

For a moment, she felt annoyed that Jacob had fooled her. But the very next moment, she thought it was none of her business, what he did and why he did. *I've got to trust him entirely with the fact that, whatever he's been doing, is for a good cause. I've got to be grateful to him because he has given me a roof over my head with full protection, care and affection. What else do I need? Of course, I'd thought, he'd told me everything about his project till date, but he still has a few secrets from me. Maybe he intends to tell me about the sounds, when the time is right, as he mentioned. I should not rush him into telling me something which he doesn't wish to. He must have reasons of his own. I must wait for the right time. I believe that Jacob is a good man and doesn't intend to bring me any harm or shame. I must give him his space. Jacob's company is all that I need right now. I owe him, unconditional love.*

She dropped and lolled on the couch and thought deeply for a few minutes. Soon the sounds of the digging stopped. She thought it would be best for her to retire to the bedroom before being seen by Jacob. She didn't want him to feel that she was meddling with his affairs. But even before she could get out of the couch, Jacob entered the cabin from outside. Upon seeing her, he was a little taken aback, but he knew this kind of situation was expected any day anytime.

'Hi there, Olivia. What's the matter? Why aren't you sleeping?' he asked, going to the washbasin and thoroughly washing his hands.

'No, Jacob, I couldn't sleep because I heard the thudding sounds again and felt a little curious. Moreover, I was amazed to see that you were not sleeping on the couch; instead, it was just a pillow out here that had seemed like you to me in the moonlight. I was stunned to see that the green bag was missing from the backyard,' she said observing that he was wearing knee-length gumshoes which were a little dirty with mud sticking to the foot of his shoes. 'So, I started to wonder if it was you who was responsible for the sounds all these nights. But I am sorry to be curious about what you have been doing. Anyway, it's none of my business to be nosy in your errands and I better mind my own business,' she confessed and started to move towards the bedroom.

'Olivia, you are a clever girl,' Jacob said. 'Come here, sit with me on the couch,' he said, holding her arms gently and guiding her with him to the couch. 'I need to show you something, please don't be annoyed with me that I kept a secret from you,' he said.

'Jacob, don't you worry. I do not want to push you. I trust you. I am sorry for having alarmed you, by snooping around in the night,' she confessed.

'Olivia,' said Jacob, caressing her cheek. 'It's not your fault. I'm doing some digging that is no way concerned with finding the treasure. I'm doing it for a different purpose and thought it was not important to you. I thought you might get used to the sounds sooner and never mind it. But it looks like I have disturbed your sleep almost every night. I am sorry,' he confessed, 'OK, come with me. I need to show you something.'

He held her hand, brought her out of the cabin and directed her towards the back of the cabin. He opened a small hidden door at the cabin's base from the back of its stilted foundation. Olivia was amazed to see the secret door and was surprised that she had never noticed it before, even though she had snooped around many times in the backyard. 'Where does this door lead to Jacob? I never noticed it.' she asked bewildered.

'Just follow me,' he said, getting into the secret door after switching his torch on. she followed him. They entered into a hole under the cabin through the secret door. Several rough stairs were made in the mud and rocks to climb down into a pit that was almost 6x6 feet wide and 15 feet deep below the cabin.

'I've been digging this pit, right at the bottom of my cabin,' he said. 'You must be wondering why I'm doing this and why I didn't tell you about it. When I find the treasure, I intend to use this hole as safe for the treasure before I hand it over to the mastermind, Roark. Also, I am digging this pit to fill it in with any junk I leave behind when I am done with my project and decide to quit this place. As you know, many people are after the treasure, and even a few men like Brayan and Gilbert, who are working with me on this project are not trustworthy. So it is my responsibility to safeguard the treasure until I relinquished it to the right person, Roark. Of course, there might be few spies of his, who would see to it that the treasure remains safe once it is found, but I need to be careful and do the right thing from my side as I have a greater responsibility in this whole mission,' said Jacob.

Olivia was listening to him intently with wide eyes, standing in the pit. 'But what about Peter? Does he know about this hole as well?' she asked.

'No, he doesn't know. But I have just assured him that I would be taking care of the treasure after it is found. Peter trusts me. Once the treasure is safely transported to Roark and I decide to quit this place, I also intend to use this pit to dump all the junk I want to leave behind. I do not want anyone else to know that I once stayed and tarried here during my errand. I am going to demolish the cabin and make everything look untouched. I do not want to attract any kind of attention from the police or the government about the shady affairs that must have happened around here,' justified Jacob.

'Right now, it's only you who knows about this basement, apart from me.' he continued. 'Initially, when you asked me to provide you with some shelter, I could not deny your request, at least after seeing your innocent, translucent, pink, flawless face. At the same time, I did not want to alarm you, as you did not know about my purpose. But in the recent past, things have moved faster and the days have become eventful, and I just couldn't come to tell you anything much. But you kept growing on me, and I started to confide in you slowly. So I guess this is the right time you knew about the source of the thudding sounds you have heard all these nights. Tomorrow, we are going on an expedition to the base of the summit, and hopefully, our plan and strategy would work, and I might need this hole under my cabin to safeguard the treasure.

Hope you are not cross with me,' he said with great concern.

'Definitely not, Jacob,' said Olivia. 'Why should I be cross with you? You have your reasons, and I believe it is in your best interest. I trust your deeds and wow! the whole thing sounds so exciting. How I wish I could accompany you in your expedition!' she said with excitement. 'But, crooked Gilbert will be around, and this idea of mine is not feasible I guess,' she said somberly.

'Don't you worry, sweetheart. Once I'm done with my mission, just the two of us will enjoy the mountain to our heart's content before I leave this place.' He assured her.

'But what about after you leave, where am I going to go?' she looked concerned.

'You? Of course, you are coming with me' he said, without a doubt and looked at her expression. She looked happy.

'Really? Do you mean it, Jacob? Oh, Jacob, I can't believe this; everything is a dream come true,' she said and hugged Jacob. He saw her sparkling blue eyes filling with tears of happiness. 'Thank God, I have finally discovered the source of the thudding and hammering sounds. From now on, I can sleep carefree even if I hear the sounds again,' she said, laughing.

'True,' said Jacob, 'but I'm sorry to have disturbed you all these nights, I didn't mean to scare you. When I tried to convince you that you were safe here, I thought you would believe me despite the sounds. I didn't want you to hear the sounds. That's why I used to do that job after midnight as I thought you would be fast asleep by then. Even if you heard them, I wanted you to think I was sleeping on the couch that could give you courage. But you are a very alert and cautious girl.' He pecked at her nose with his finger, smiling. They realized that they were having all this conversation in the dark hole at the cabin's base, in the middle of the night.

'Jacob, show me what you have done here with the pit,' she asked with curiosity.

'Nothing much. I have dug a pit, that's all,' Jacob said, showing her around with the help of a torch. It was quite a big pit.

'Jacob, you have done this job all alone. I could have helped you with this. All these days I was free and didn't know how to spend my time. Do you intend to dig it further or this is it?' she asked.

'I intended to make it a little deeper, maybe another two to three feet more. But now it looks like it's not possible because tomorrow we are going to kick start our expedition to the base of the summit. I guess I'll have to manage with whatever I've got here,' Jacob said.

'Ok, then, when you go on your expedition tomorrow, I can dig this pit further for you,' she said.

'No, don't. Don't take the trouble of physically straining yourself. You are a delicate girl, and this kind of job doesn't agree with you,' he said.

'Try me,' she said, challenging him.

'As you wish,' said Jacob. The two of them chuckled. They immediately went back and slept in the cabin without spending any more time chatting because the next day would be a really big day for Jacob.

CHAPTER 11

~~~~~ ☐ ~~~~~

The next morning, Jacob was up early, as he had to meet up with his associates who were going to accompany and assist him in the expedition for a treasure hunt. He was buoyant, full of hopes because he already possessed detailed information about the location of the ice cased hidden caves containing the mighty treasure. Until now, everything had been propitious. He remembered the faint shimmering light of Georgina's spirit that had appeared high above on Mount Jett at the base of its summit, indicating the possible spot where they could start digging the hard ice to find the caves within. He felt more confident and optimistic than ever.

Jacob was fervid to discover the caves and be enlightened by their treasure trove. He wondered, how stark and unfathomable the caves could have been to have protected the treasure from the ferocious natural calamities of the hicksville. He couldn't wait to begin the expedition, but before that, he had to make suitable preparations for the same, as it would be a frenetic and dangerous adventure. He also had to prepare his associates by giving them proper instructions regarding the expedition's proceedings. Though Gilbert, Adrian and Darby were local people, au fait with the mountain, they were untrained and crude adventure loving people and thus required some tips on mountaineering and other aspects concerning the treasure hunt.

Olivia was still sleeping because of her disturbed sleep the previous night. Jacob decided not to wake her up. He noshed on some eggs and coffee for breakfast, and as he stepped out of the cabin, Olivia woke up and hollered for him. Knowing she had woken up, he came back inside to kiss her goodbye.

'Olivia, don't you ever try anything knavish today at the cabin. It's better if you left the underground pit alone. It's not your cup of tea to resume the digging out there. The last thing I expect is for you to get hurt,' he advised.

'Jacob, it's not fair,' she said, pouting her lips feigning annoyed expression. 'First of all, you won't let me go with you on the expedition; secondly, you object me from meddling with the pit below the cabin. At least you can let me do that, right? It's so exciting to be involved in your adventure. I swear, I will be careful not to get hurt. Please....? If only my ex were not involved in this affair, you couldn't have stopped me accompanying you in your expedition. Even if you had denied, I would have followed you,' she said disappointingly, cursing Gilbert.

Jacob smiled, sensing her great interest and enthusiasm. He also felt sorry for her that she did not have anything else to do, instead, experience boredom at the lonely cabin. 'Ok then,' Jacob said, feigning anger, 'you are a reckless, adamant girl. You can do whatever you want. But take care of yourself. While you meddle with the basement, do not forget to wear my gumshoes to protect your legs and ankles. You must wear my leather gloves to protect your delicate hands as well,' he cautioned.

Olivia cheered, 'Oh! Thank you so much, Jacob! You are a real sweetheart. Your generosity strikes me as wonderful,' she cuddled him. 'I'm so happy. Though it's not a big deal, you have decided to allow me to be a small part of your project so that I could contribute whatever possible from my side. I'll do all I can to make the underground pit quite spacious enough for whatever you want to use it for later on.'

'Honestly, I feel so silly for having dug this pit, even before finding the treasure. I don't even know whether the mission will be successful. Already, I have made a pit to hide the treasure in, with a secret door to top-up. I think I have tried to hatch the eggs before the hen.'

'Never mind, Jacob. It indicates you are prophesying a mighty treasure with great optimism and confidence. Moreover, if you couldn't get your hands on the treasure, you can always use this pit to dump all the junk you want to leave behind before we leave,' she soothed.

'Yeah, that's true, that was my intention too,' he nodded. He wished Olivia good luck and took leave of her for the day. She wished him good luck too and said she would miss him.

The six men gathered by the White River, to chew over how to implement the mission's procedures and proceedings. As Gilbert and Brayan had stayed away from the ritual, Jacob explained to them how the ritual was executed and accomplished; how Georgina's spirit had loomed by the base of the summit on the east face as a blazing white light. Gilbert and Brayan were spellbound, listening to everything about the event. Though they were dismayed by the fact that they were not allowed to partake in the ritual, they had to accept it because they did not want to put their lives at stake even after being warned. They wanted to get their hands on the treasure by hook or crook; so they decided to play safe.

After learning everything about the ritual and Georgina's spirit, Brayan and Gilbert agreed that Glinda had performed a dinkum ritual and felt relieved that they kept themselves away from it and saved their lives. But at least they were contented, like dogs with two tails that, they were going to be allowed to participate in the treasure hunt and rewarded handsomely if the mission was successful.

For the moment they thought it was the best option to do precisely as Jacob and Peter instructed because Jacob and Peter were the two men of essence, who knew more than anyone else about the hidden chest and its location.

Jacob looked at his associates and said. 'We will get our show on the road, early tomorrow by daybreak, so that, by sunrise, we can reach the tree line. From there upwards to the base of the summit, will be a bit of mountaineering, and we have no idea how tough it's gonna be. So we need to endow ourselves well with all the indispensable equipment and tools. Of course, food, water, tents and sleeping bags will be among the major inclusions. We don't know whether we may have to tarry out there on top for a couple of days, digging and exploring, until we find the treasure.' All men listened to him carefully.

'You have been fixed with the daily wage to help us with the treasure hunt,' said Peter, addressing Gilbert, Adrian and Darby. 'So, if at all, and when we are successful in finding the treasure, Jacob will be keeping the treasure with him, until it is consigned to the mastermind, Roark,' he said, while the three local men looked a little disenchanted. 'But you will be paid handsomely for your support, beyond the shadow of a doubt. Maybe you will get a fraction of the treasure as well, you never know! It all depends on how faithful and true-blue you remain in your work, and how happy will Roark be with you guys. Roark does not entertain double-crossing people. If any of us tried to act smart, we are finished. This truth is something that we must bear in mind, above all,' he cautioned.

The three local men shivered, envisaging that this was all a very tricky sitch. The three locals had tried to forage through the mountain for the treasure earlier but in vain. Now, they had offered to help these hi-tech outsiders who had all the expertise and brainpower, for a daily wage. Still, Gilbert was chomping at the bit, to get some share in the treasure. He was already building a castle in the air. It was inevitable that they toed the line at the moment. They thought something was better than nothing and hence agreed to play it by the book, neatly as Jacob and Peter instructed.

Jacob gave them the list of things and equipment they needed to fetch for the expedition. Peter gave them some money to buy the equipment. Jacob, Brayan and Peter, already had their equipment as they were an important part of the mission and had arrived on the mountain well-prepared. They all dispersed deciding to bunch up by the White River the next day, to embark on the expedition towards the base of the summit on the east face.

Olivia lavishly packed food for Jacob in several packets, for his expedition. She did it meticulously with great interest and packed sandwiches, fruits, extra high protein cheese, energy drinks, etc. She felt optimistic, with the whole affair: how she wished she could accompany him! But Jacob had denied the idea as it was not advisable. She also did her bit with the packing of his rucksack, with all the equipment needed for mountaineering, digging and metal detecting. She knew that this would be a great adventure and that she would miss it.

'Jacob, I know I'm going to pine for you while you are away. I hope you find the treasure and rush back to me at the earliest,' said Olivia, hoping for the best.

'Sure, Rose, I hope so, and I'll try my best to return at the earliest with flying colours. I cannot stay away from you for long as well.' He ensured a kiss on her pink lips, that gave her some frail consolation.

The previous day she had tried digging the pit below the cabin but had found it back-breaking due to the impeding rocks and roots. So she had quit the idea for the time being. Still, she did not want to give it all up. She wanted to be of some help to Jacob in any possible way, as she believed, every little bit would come handy in his project. The two of them hugged amorously and bid a warm and solicitous goodbye to each other.

As instructed and guided by Jacob and Peter,

the other men had prepared themselves with all the necessary equipment. With all the inspiration bestowed upon them by Jacob and Peter, they got mentally ready for any hardships in the course of their journey. Even though Gilbert had once managed to reach the base of the summit, he had done so with sleazy procedures, without any prerequisite skills. Moreover, it was on the south face that he had ventured, which was much easier than the east face. As Gilbert was a bit wet behind the ears, he had hopelessly returned, not knowing how to proceed further, being in an abominable sitch. This time he felt more confident, as Jacob and Peter had provided them with valuable instructions and equipment. He also knew that Peter and Jacob would save his neck if any mischance happened with him during mountaineering.

They all assembled by the bank of White River. There, they forged ahead with their expedition on their horses towards the timberline. The daylight had drifted to twilight by the time they reached the timberline at the height of 10,000 feet from the sea level. They rested there for the night. They resumed their journey, the next day before sunrise. This time they trekked by foot. They left their horses in the mercy of a shepherd, by tempting him with a substantial emolument, if he took proper care of the animals till they returned. They promised him they would return at the earliest.

The terrain above the timberline was quite bleak, ice studded, rugged, and rocky. They had to climb at least 3000 feet more to reach the base of the summit, where the white light of Georgina's spirit had presented itself. Initially, they did some rock mountaineering, while they had to do ice mountaineering at some other places; managed to do so as they had a different set of equipment for both. They also formed a rope team to support each other in some areas. Jacob and Peter were exceptionally proficient and protective about their team and furthered the other men to crusade methodically, under their steadfast governance.

By owl light, they hit the base of the summit. Two days had passed just like that, trekking and mountaineering. Still, they were thrilled and enkindled with glee that they had managed to get as far as the base of the summit without any untoward troubles or hassles during their endeavour. They were bursting with hopes and energy.

The mountain peak was another 1000 feet above the base of the summit. But they didn't have to worry about reaching that height because the caves were hidden in the base of the summit as guaranteed by Glinda.

As Jacob gazed in the twilight, at the silhouette of the peak from its base, against the silvery starspeckled sky, he was overwhelmed with ecstasy and emotional turmoil. At the same time, he felt profoundly and powerfully connected with it in the chill of the breezy night. Amazingly, it was an experience of rhapsody, very much positive and different from his experiences of his other expeditions. Then and there, he made up his mind to reach Mount Jett's peak in this expedition. After all this challenging endeavour, he had to reach the peak at least once to fulfil his spiritual urge. As it was already nightfall, they had to rest, and he decided to effectuate his wish of reaching the zenith, the crowning point of the mountain, at the first blush of dawn all alone.

They dug some ice by the lee side of the ridge where Jacob indicated, to form a pockmark that could shelter them for the night, among the rain shadow of ice-covered rocks. They had dinner and rested in the cavern-like area they had created. Before they slept, the local men appreciated Jacob and Peter for their skills and aid.

The next day was going to be another action-packed day. As Jacob stretched out in his sleeping bag, he visualized Olivia and was a little worried about whether she was fine and thriving well, all alone. He smiled at the thought of her trying to dig the pit at the bottom of the cabin with her tender untoughened body and delicate hands. He reminisced the deep hug they had shared before leaving and felt warm in his heart. 'Olivia, I miss you. I'll return to you as soon as possible, with triumph,' he murmured a promise that no one around him heard, as all the other men were sleeping like a top.

Jacob woke up with a fresh mind at the first peep of the day. As he made out of his sleeping bag, he shuddered due to the low temperatures at that altitude, supplemented by mild snowfall and cool breeze, rendering the weather, brutal. Still, the warmth in his heart and high spirits, helped him withstand the severe climatic conditions. He related his spiritual and emotional connections with the whole affair at Mount Jett with the moral support proffered by Glinda and her ritual. His associates also were in good spirits. As planned, Jacob informed his associates about his interest in reaching the peak; all alone, to a steep height of another 1000 feet above their location. He relinquished his leadership to Peter for the time being.

Peter said they would wait for Jacob to return, but Brayan and Gilbert said, waiting was a waste of time; moreover, it was not a place for frolicking or recreation. They said they could instantly start digging the ice if Jacob gave them the proper location. Jacob agreed to it because anyway Peter was going to be with them to guide, and of course, it would take a long time to dig all the ice that could be thickly covering the caves' entrance. He thought he could make it back by then.

Jacob studied the location as per Glinda's instructions that she had given at dawn after the ritual. He located the spot exactly where the star of Georgina's spirit was seen during the ceremony, using his compass and instructed them to start digging in the pockmark that they had created for their shelter. He made headway with his escapade, alone towards the peak.

'Be careful, Jacob. Watch your steps,' cautioned Peter. Jacob assured him that he would remain safe and return to join them back in a jiffy.

For a moment, Jacob lost his confidence when he looked up at the steep pitch to the summit. He was well equipped and made up his mind to pursue the attempt, no matter what. He knew he had to do this, once in his lifetime, and now was the right time. He commenced his venture with great zeal. He did one hell of an ice mountaineering which was quite challenging and demanding, finally managing to reach the summit.

His heart filled with joy as he stepped on the highest point of Mount Jett. He felt like on top of the world as his eyes sparkled with tears to see the array of Spruce jungle ranges spread all around him with the terrain of glaciers blessing him with all their celestial powers. He truly got a buzz out of this venture and thought this was heaven on earth. The peak had a small flat area around it, and he lingered there, strolling and viewing the surrounding mountainous high-lands and feasting his eyes with their beauty and splendour. He felt calm within his heart and took in the tantalizing sunrise from the peak of Mount Jett. It was the most practically blissful moment that he had ever experienced.

He sat there for an hour or so in a trance, meditating and rejoicing the morning sun. He ate a high-protein cheese sandwich, boosted himself with energy drink and an apple for his late breakfast, sitting on the Zenith of Mount Jett. It felt like home! The whole treasure hunt project did not seem important at that moment of divinity. He closed his eyes, meditated for a while, even forgetting his existence on earth, and everything else seemed secondary. He stood up and laundered over the summit, not wanting to go back down to the real world. He wanted to settle there forever and ever.

As he laundered for some time on the summit scrutinizing the area, he was shocked to see two dead human bodies, lying there frozen. He felt disturbed seeing their plight. He guessed they might be bodies of some men who could have landed on the summit chasing the treasure and got ended up there, dead. He didn't want to wind up like them. Suddenly he remembered Olivia, his mission and all the reasons why he was here on Mount Jett. He decided it was time to climb down the summit, go back and join the others. Before he could realize what was happening, the ice gave way under his feet, and there he fell in a wide and deep crevice with no one around to rescue him!

~ ~ ~ ~

Meanwhile, Olivia was all alone, feeling aloof and lonely, after Jacob left on his expedition. To spend her deserted crazy time, she thought of digging the pit further. The first day, Olivia tried doing some digging, after Jacob left. But somehow, she failed to proceed with the job as she felt gloomy without him around and not knowing when he would be back. She kept praying God to make his mission successful. She didn't feel hungry, either. She strolled around the cabin. She tried reading books to overcome her boredom and anxiety, but she felt restless and couldn't focus on doing anything worthy. She was truly worried and anxious about Jacob and his safety and his mission's success.

God, please protect Jacob for me, from any catastrophe that could arise in the course of his expedition. I can't bear to think that he might get hurt during the process and might never return to me. Already I've got a star-crossed past. But this time, God, you need to help me by taking care of Jacob and seeing to it that nothing wrong happens with him.

She could not concentrate on her work, on reading or anything for that matter for almost a day. She kept imagining, where would Jacob be at the moment? And what was he doing? Later she felt stupid about herself, for wasting her time wool-gathering, brooding over unnecessary thoughts and doubts aimlessly, to which there were no answers at that moment. So she decided to do something useful.

Jacob had informed her, it would take a minimum of one week or more, depending on the circumstances, for his return. She wished he would return within a couple of days with flying colours. She often came out of the cabin impulsively, to see if he had returned. She laughed at herself for her silly behaviour. She finally decided to go about with the digging at the bottom of the cabin, to do something worthwhile.

Olivia, you need to focus. She cautioned herself. *If your love for Jacob is truly worthy, he is verily going to come back to you. I know you do not care about the treasure or the fortune. It's Jacob whom you care about, and your true love for him will protect him. Now get on with your work. You are one meagre delicate thing, and you need a lot of time to do the required digging, perfectly as per Jacob's requirements. At least you can do, this one small contribution towards his mission.*

On the second day, she opened the green bag after breakfast and selected the necessary equipment. She also studied other tools. She studied the metal detector, but as it was a hi-end one, she failed to recall its operating procedures that Jacob had shown her a few days back. She wore gloves and gumshoes. Switching on the torch, she climbed down the pit through the secret door. Of course, she did not forget to take the pistol with her, which Jacob had given before leaving, for her safety. She felt thrilled to realize that the pistol was loaded and proudly carried it down into the pit.

She did quite an appreciable work, digging, on the second and third day. That made her very tired and starved. She felt hungry and ate well as well. She was determined to complete her part of the job efficiently. As she was not used to that kind of laborious work, it took her longer than expected, to finish the job. By the end of the third day, she had accomplished digging another two feet deep. She sat there in the basement enjoying the entertaining thoughts about Jacob and the good times they'd had together in the recent past after she'd met him. She had no notion that he had reached the peak of Mount Jett and had fallen into a deep, wide crevice with no one around to help him.

She tried using the metal detector again, just for fun, to see if she could descry anything of interest. She tried remembering the operating procedures Jacob had demonstrated to her once and tried searching the pit with it. When she got suspicious that something was there, she dug the area again to find a small metal vase and could not make out whether it was of virtue. Still, it was fun.

Finally, at the end of the fifth day, she had turned

the pit into a perfect cuboid with a neat base and walls, and now, it looked more like a cellar than a hole, perfect for storing anything safely in secret. *Nobody would ever guess that there is a secret cache below this cabin. It's perfectly hidden, like the hidden caves of Mount Jett!!* She thought gleefully and felt amused.

CHAPTER 12

~~~~~ 〇 ~~~~~

Under Peter's guidance and supervision, the rest of the men on treasure hunt started to dig at the wall of the thick, sturdy concretion of ice they suspected was casing the caves' entrance. As they kept digging, thrusting, scraping and shovelling the ice, they saw more ice and only ice and nothing else. They had almost dug two feet wide and six feet deep inside the wall of ice, in turns, and still couldn't see any opening or even a rock, but were only confronted by thick hardened ice.

Gilbert felt hopeless, 'Guys, I think this is leading to nowhere. I guess, the stupid witch Glinda, has undoubtedly taken a mocking chance with us. She has given us a bum steer. I cannot take any more of this nonsense,' he said in disgust. 'The other day at the timberline, even after strenuous attempt, we could not find the Buddha idol, and it was so discouraging and disappointing. Today, it's looking anticlimactic as well, even after putting in our best efforts. This is all because of Glinda's stupidity. Or, is Jacob playing a game with us by giving us a wrong location?' he doubted, restless.

'Stop nitpicking and being fussy, Gilbert. Why would Jacob do that? Try to think straight. We need each other to make the mission a success. We all need to pin our hopes on each other because it's a teamwork. Most importantly, Glinda is a genuine person, and we need to trust her,' said Peter, irritated with Gilbert's resentful attitude, looking at him with contempt. 'Whatever effort we have put in till now is negligible. It's nothing. Anybody would have found the treasure by now if it was easy; a five-finger exercise. It would help if you were composed with enough forbearance, as there is still a long way to go before we accomplished what we are here for,' he tried to nudge Gilbert with some sense.

'Do you think this is the right spot where we are thrusting?' asked Brayan. 'What if we found nothing but a big rock mocking at us at the end of all the struggle out here?' he asked hopelessly.

'For the love of God! Trust, dedication, confidence and patience are all we need at the moment to boost our pursuit,' sangfroid mannered Peter said. 'So it will be better, if we inculcate at least some of it to reap the benefits of our attempt otherwise everything would look pointless and forlorn, and our energy would drain fallaciously,' he cautioned.

The men continued digging the ice, relentlessly. By late afternoon, they had drilled almost thirty feet deep into the wall of the ice, forming a passageway kind of route enclosed by thick ice walls and a roof. After another foot of excavation, they felt reassured, when they saw the ice gave way and opened into a small round chamber among the rocks. The section looked like a small entrance to the mighty caves within, and that charged them with hopes, redeeming their expectations. All of them looked at each other with optimism and cheered with happiness.

'Whoa! This den looks like the entrance to the hidden caves. After all, it isn't discouraging I guess,' exclaimed Gilbert, 'and where is Jacob? Why hasn't he returned yet?'

All the explorers entered the small rocky cave-like hollow. As it was quite dark inside, they all had to use their torches. They were excited to see that this void-like area led to another cavern, deeper to it.

'Oh, my goodness! I am sure we are standing in the hidden caves now. Looks like, all the information given by Glinda is legit,' said Brayan thrilled. 'God must know how many and how deep the caves are! And where could be the hidden treasure?!' The adventure seemed promising and rosy. All the men hankered inside the cavernous spaces with rejuvenated gusto, full of hopes.

Peter was worried the passage they'd created could get occluded, due to more snowfall in the nights and so decided to track their course. He instructed Darby and Adrian to fix and secure a rope at the entrance of the ice passage and take it along with them on their route as they moved inside the caves deeper and deeper so that when they wished to return, they could easily find their way back to the outside. He said that the rope would also guide Jacob to join them when he returned from the summit. Everybody thought it was a brilliant idea. *But Jacob should have returned by now,* thought Peter, a little concerned.

They proceeded from one cave to another and were thrilled to see the gaping caverns' intricate formation and infrastructure. On the inside, it was quite ambiguous, as some caves led to other caves in different directions and the whole sector was so mysterious and resembled a maze runner. They did not know in which direction to proceed, to search for the treasure. Of course, at that moment, they believed that Glinda had given them a proper location to dig for the caves, but it was not all and not enough. They realized, just finding the hidden caves was not good enough to discover and retrieve the treasure.

The rate at which the caves divided in an alveolate fashion, seemed like it would take weeks to months to explore the whole area in itself. They wondered how much more time it would take to locate the hidden treasure. It was too much of a puzzle to fathom the immense caves, which could not be possible in a few days. They had brought food that could last for 15 days. After looking at the enormous and magnificent cavernous hideout, they doubted, if they could complete their mission within a fortnight. They wished Jacob would join them sooner as they believed he was well clued up on the ways to explore further.

~ ~ ~ ~

If Jacob's situation were all ok and hunky-dory, he would have joined the others by then. But Jacob was grappling with a whole new ball-game, which the others were not aware of. Peter was anxious for Jacob. *What could be the reason for Jacob's delay? Is he safe? Something seems amiss,* thought Peter. Still, he speculated that Jacob would be okay because he knew Jacob was quick-witted and skilled, a person with great potential, which Peter had observed during their expedition, up the mountain. He knew that Jacob was exceptionally savvy and wouldn't take any kind of grave risk that could hurt him and that he would venture, only if he were sure of his know-how and moxie. But Peter failed to imagine that, somehow this time, Jacob had become too emotional on reaching the summit and had heedlessly fallen into a wide, deep crevice. Peter was in charge of the task. He thought it was not wise to stop and wait for Jacob's return as they were already short of time and food, but had much to explore and accomplish in that colossal, cavernous place.

The explorers were bowled over by the alveolate inestimable magnitude of the caves. They were at a nonplus, viewing the beauty of the caves within. They also conjectured that long back the caves must have been inhabited by humanity and spruced up as per the requirement. They also found several rock carvings and paintings on the rough walls substantiating the same. Of course, that established Jungle Jett's inhabitance with his gang in the caves, long ago. They were also shocked when they stumbled upon several frozen mummified bodies and skeletons of the dead people, here and there. They guessed the bodies belonged to the treasure hunters who might have attempted chasing the treasure years ago in vain or maybe the bodies belonged to some members of Jungle Jett's gang as well, who might have stayed back on Mount Jett.

At some places, they found glittery star-like spots on the roofs of the caves with icicles, here and there. Peter said they were glowing insects, which meant there was oxygen supply inside the caves.

'Certainly, there must be some chinks or apertures in the rocks, from where the air could be entering into the caves,' said Brayan.

'Of course, that's a possibility,' said Peter as they progressed slowly, keeping their route towards the west for nearly 50 yards through the cavernous passages and foramina in the rocks and eventually found themselves in a more oversized vestibule resembling a great hall. They were starstruck to see that this hall was furnished and remodelled with rocky chairs, beds, dining tables, etc., all dusty and cob-webbed, but everything was made in rocks and fixed as if someone had carved and sculptured the rocks and transformed the place into a utility room.

'Wow, this is incredible!' exclaimed Gilbert. 'This explains Jungle Jett might have spent time here in this vestibule with his gang, while he was hiding among these caves, after every burglary. Jungle Jett and his gang must be highly skilled and nimble-fingered, to have created a beautifully furnished, desolate den for themselves during those tough days, in the wild. They must be quite intelligent and truly adventurous,' he appreciated, while the others were speechless, looking at its grandeur.

~ ~ ~ ~

The scenario with Jacob was relatively discrete. When the ice gave way at his feet on the summit, he fell into a wide crevice and landed on a snow-laden platform a few yards deep down. He was shocked and panicked he might get trapped there and die without anyone to help him, similar to the frozen corpses he had encountered on top of the summit. He looked up and saw that the mountain's summit was not too high from where he had landed. He evaluated that he could climb back onto the summit, without much difficulty as he had his rucksack with him and hence all the equipment needed. He felt a bit of solace after reassuring himself that he could somehow manage to mingle with the others and join hands in the excavation. He wondered how much progress the others would have made, by then. He couldn't have reckoned that they could be already sauntering in the hidden caves, as the caves were a mystery to him as well. He kind of felt guilty because he knew that the others needed his help and guidance, but he was here in a deep ice pit, hopelessly trying to find a way back. *I shouldn't let myself and others down,* he decided with hope against hope, keeping his fingers crossed.

As he slowly tried to raise himself on his knees and stand on his feet, the ice beneath him gave way again!! *Gracious! No, no, no! This can't be happening! Not fair!* He panicked. He was too dazed as he fell deeper and deeper into the crevice. He slid through the twists and turns and ice caverns, at places. He did not know what was happening to him at that moment. He went on and on, gliding and slipping, smoothly and speedily through the ice holes and cracks and slits and pipes. It was so slippery that he couldn't even try and hold on to anything. Even if he had managed to hold on to something, it was impossible to climb back, as he was getting implanted deeper and deeper in the heart of Mount Jett.

He gave up hopes because he knew that he was embroiled and getting boxed in among the glaciers and would never be able to come back to the light of the outside world. He accepted that his life was finished and froze like a trapped animal. For a moment, Olivia's face flashed in front of his eyes, and he felt depressed that he was never going to see her again. At that moment, he realized that he was deeply in love with her. He had no choice but to yield to his fate.

Finally, after a long slide of about 15 to 20 minutes, he fell on a broader space that was more of a scaffold. The surrounding was quite dark but slightly visible due to the light, sparkling through the ice. He realized that he was not much hurt except for a few abrasions here and there. *God! Where on earth am I? How could I be so careless? Oh, the magnificent Mount Jett, I climbed on to your summit to get your blessings for my venture, to hunt the treasure, to unravel and unburden you of your long lost secrets and what have you done to me? I am embedded deep inside your heart, and how am I gonna get out of here? How is anybody going to find me?* He wondered, bewildered. He felt miserable that all his efforts had been rendered meaningless by his mere carelessness and bad luck.

He switched on his torch and found that the floor was rocky but covered with sleet. He cleared the snow and the sleet and saw nothing but rock everywhere on the ground and around him. He tried standing up very slowly, hoping the ground wouldn't collapse neath his feet again. When he confirmed that the ground was firm under him, he stood up confidently and studied the area. He concluded that it was some lonely void in the mountain, and there was no way he could get out of there. He plopped down for some time, trying to figure out what to do next. There was some amount of oxygen available inside the hole for now. Still, he was scared it soon might become deficient, if the cracks and holes and slits got covered by snow and ice, which of course, could happen within no time due to the snowfall and freezing temperatures at the summit.

I shouldn't accept the fact that I'm gonna die here in this hole. I shouldn't waste any more of my time. Every cloud has a silver lining, he thought optimistically and started to study the pit walls and suddenly noticed a small aperture at one corner. The gap was just wide enough for one person to wriggle through, *but where does it lead to? What if I got lost in the deeper, secret dark crevices of the mountain? The crevices and the pits unknown to the outside world! The holes that have never seen daylight!* He focused on the crack with his torch and decided to at least wriggle through it and see where it led. If it led to nowhere, he thought he could always return through the same crack back to the scaffold where he had fallen from above. *Let me at least give a try.*

As he slid into the crack, he noticed that the gap was narrow initially and to his relief became wider and wider as he crawled further through it. *I'm here on this mountain to hunt for the treasure, but now, I'm in the middle of nowhere, hunting for a way to get out! How pathetic of me!* He squirmed sardonically in distress. *I should have just stayed back, sticking to others, instead of trying to reach the summit. Who could have known that I may have to face such grave consequences?* He regretted. He soon came into a broader, wintry dark space between several jagged rocks and boulders, where he still felt was warmer compared to the outside.

He tried finding if that space had a way out. He saw a medium-sized boulder of rock at one corner in the dark. There he was alarmed to see another frozen mummified dead body with its back resting on the boulder. *Am I going to end up like this too?* He felt like there was a giant chasm between him and the outside world. He felt claustrophobic and fidgeted with oppression. On closer look, he could discern that the dead body was that of a woman; *a woman's corpse!.* Her dress was intact but all crinkled and scrunched up and stiffly frozen. He recalled what Glinda had whispered in his ears after the ritual and instinctively examined the body to look for a clue. To his great amazement of a lifetime, he saw the tattoo with Jett's name on the left forearm of the woman's body!

Gracious me! She is GEORGINA!! Here is GEORGINA's body!! What a pleasant revelation, a fortuitous discovery! I can't believe it! The tattoo is the clue that Glinda had whispered into my ears while she had blessed me! Oh my Gosh! Oh my Gosh! This is brilliant! A dream come true, a serendipitous twist in the tale! It indicates I have fallen into the hidden caves from above and truly blessed by Mount Jett. Glinda said Georgina never went away with her daughter Cynthia; instead, she went back to the mountains and never returned. Here is her body with her spirit guarding the treasure all these years. It's truly baffling and gratifying. Jacob kissed the corpse on its forehead overwhelmed, while tears welled in his eyes with happiness and bliss. *If Georgina's body is here, then the treasure must also be somewhere around here!!* He became vigilant and started to ferret around in the vicinity with his heart thudding.

Something flashed in his head in a well-timed manner, and he decided to move the boulder aside, against which Georgina's body was resting. The boulder was quite tough to move, was stuck tightly to the ground, making it impossible to push it aside with his bare hands. He lifted Georgina's body and put her aside. He used all his strength and pushed the boulder, but the boulder did not stir an inch. He used his pry bar and tried technically, which helped him dislodge the boulder and roll it aside.

He pushed aside the boulder from its original position to reveal quite a big triangular-shaped opening in the wall behind it. His hopes got lifted. He focused on the triangular opening with his torch and slowly entered through it. His eyes widened as he stared at something gloriously seated in the darkest corner of the inner hole. The Brass Chest! The highly coveted treasure!

He just couldn't believe that this was all truly happening. He pinched himself to confirm that he wasn't dreaming. This was the treasure they were searching for. Destiny had gotten him there directly to it, from above the summit. He felt truly blessed! Jacob saw that the brass chest's lid was fastened with a huge lock. He couldn't wait to unlock it and explore the chest's interior, but, *where is the key?!*

He brought the heavy chest out of the hole, pushing it slowly with difficulty. He searched Georgina's body again with the hopes of finding the key. To his gratification, he found the diamond necklace hidden in her bosom, another clue that Glinda had given him while she'd whispered into his ears; the visions she had seen of Georgina! There was a key tied to the necklace to his astonishment; a bonus discovery. Everything was happening miraculously. He tried opening the lock by using that key and of course, it got unlocked. He lifted the brass chest's lid and was more than amazed to see that the brass chest was full of glittery ornaments made of diamonds, gold, pearls and precious stones; all of Georgina's favourite jewellery, the loot!! A massive treasure!!

He was ecstatic with his discovery but,.... *how am I gonna get out of this secluded bolt-hole? How am I gonna carry this heavy brass chest all alone?* He decided to leave the treasure there for some time; try and find a way out of the hideout first. He locked the brass chest; safely kept the key and the diamond necklace with him.

He now believed that he was in some remote corner of the mighty caves and needed to find an existing way out, the entrance on the east face from inside! If he tried his best, he thought it was even possible to meet the other men from the opposite direction. He looked around for more cracks and crevices in the rocky area among the boulders. He found one big gap towards the east and decided to follow it because the east face was where the cave entrance was located. He secured a rope at the opening of the hole where the treasure was hidden, so he could track it back to reach the treasure chest. As he pursued his way, passing through the cavernous passages and tunnels and slits, he was brought into bigger caves, as expected. He moved further towards the east, bringing the thin rope along with him. Still, he had to change directions at places due to the caves' crazy assembly. It was all so exciting, and he couldn't believe he had found the treasure! He just couldn't wait to report the success to Peter, Glinda and Olivia.

After trudging, crawling and jostling for nearly 400 yards through the caves in the east direction, he landed in the more significant cavernous area resembling a great hall that looked inhabited and remodelled centuries ago. He had secured the other end of the rope a few feet at the rear as it was not long enough. He was enthralled to see the hall furnishings with paintings on its walls. At the moment, he did not have any sense of time. He still couldn't believe that he had found the treasure. As he sat on a rocky bench to relax in the great hall, he imagined himself to be Jungle Jett himself, luxuriously relaxing in his cavernous hide-out. Jacob smiled at his silly imagination.

He suddenly became alert because he'd heard indistinct voices echoing through the caves. For a moment, he sat captivated because he imagined that the rocks and the figures on the painted walls were trying to speak to him, trying to narrate all the caves' hidden stories. He was entranced but soon pulled himself together and tried to perceive the present reality. *'Good God! It is the best destiny I could have ever had!* He thought, expecting to see the other men sooner! Of course, he was right! He saw Peter and Brayan emerging from another cavernous area into the great hall. The trio stood still and spellbound seeing each other, like in a dream.

'Holy shit! When did you return, Jacob?' asked Peter, approaching him and hugging Jacob affectionately. 'I am so relieved to see you back. Did you manage to reach the crown of Mount Jett?' he asked curiously.

'Yes, of course, I did. I got truly blessed,' said Jacob. The other men of the team also joined the trio and were happy to see Jacob.

'Was it easy for you to find us from the caves' entrance?' asked Peter curiously. 'Did you follow the rope we'd secured at the entrance?' Jacob didn't know what to say, and Peter continued, 'Look, Jacob, we have found the caves as per Glinda's instructions. Now we need to find the treasure. The caves are enigmatic, and it might take days to weeks for us to explore every nook and corner. I'm worried that we don't have enough food and water to last long. So let's do the recce for now; maybe we'll have to go back and return sometime later with enough supplies,' he said, looking a little concerned. 'At least we know where the caves are for the moment but didn't expect them to be so galactic and elephantine,' he sighed.

'Peter, you will be surprised to listen to my story!' Said Jacob. 'When I reached the summit, it was the blissful time of my life. But heedlessly, I fell into a wide crevice that fortunately brought me directly to the caves underneath, even without, me trying to find the caves' entrance. I didn't have to join you through the east entrance you discovered. I am coming from inside the caves to join you all'. Everyone looked at him in surprise, not grasping what Jacob meant. 'It was a queer experience. But the best part is that…. I found the treasure; the brass chest along with Georgina's frozen mummified body!' he said overwhelmed, while the others almost had a fit; unable to digest what Jacob had just said.

Holy shit,…hope you are not joking! Exclaimed the others, looking stunned and baffled. 'Where is the brass chest? Why don't you take us there right away? Did you also find Buddha idol?' asked Brayan.

'Of course, I'm not joking. I indeed found the brass chest of treasure. But I haven't found Buddha idol. I have left the brass chest back where I found it as I didn't know the way out and couldn't carry it alone. It's quite a distance from here. It's already late in the night now, I guess. I'm starving, and we need to eat and rest a bit. Look at you. How spent you all look! So, we will have dinner first, rest here for the night. Tomorrow at dawn, I will take you all to the treasure,' said Jacob. Peter agreed, but Brayan and Gilbert looked at Jacob, suspiciously.

'Don't you worry, guys,' said Jacob. 'I sure-fire

will take you there. It's a heavy chest, and I need your help to carry it out and down the mountain. I don't have any intention of cheating anyone and of course, expect the same from you. If you keep this in mind, all of us will benefit.' The others kept silent as there was no other go.

'Did you open the chest?' asked Brayan.

'No, it has a huge lock fastened to it, and I couldn't find the key,' he lied, to be on the safer side at that moment. Brayan felt a little comforted. Jacob did not mention the rope he'd secured to track back the treasure. He did not utter anything about the directions to reach the treasure. He kept the details to himself for the time being because he did not want anyone to try anything mischievous that night. They all had dinner and rested for the night, electrified with Jacob's story and accomplishment.

Next day, he took all the men to the spot where the brass chest was hidden, following the rope he'd fastened. He produced the key as if he'd just found it upon searching Georgina's corpse and opened the brass chest. They were enthralled to see the brass chest and its contents which he fastened again with the lock. They were fascinated to see Georgina's body and couldn't believe their eyes. They all carried the chest and Georgina's body, to the east entrance of the caves at the base of the summit and were much delighted that they were lucky enough to locate the hidden treasure, within a few days. Jacob had decided to hand over Georgina's body to Glinda. He knew Glinda would be pleased to see Georgina's body; would be delighted to give Georgina a respectable funeral.

They hurried back to the timberline. Though it was one heck of a job bringing down the chest, there was nothing that could have stopped them. They found their horses waiting for them, being taken good care of, by the appointed shepherd.

Jacob, Peter and Brayan paid the local men their wages along with some diamonds and pearls from the brass chest as consolation and told them to be satisfied with that and wait for Roark to pay them handsomely later. Jacob did not forget to make a note of what he gave the local men out of the chest; he needed to report it to Wolfe later on, to maintain the transparency of the mission. The three local men went on their way towards their respective villages. Darby and Adrian were more than satisfied as they had received more than they expected and happy that they would be receiving more from Roark, later on.

Gilbert was kind of happy; still, a little disappointed with what he had received. Though he had received well enough, he was a bit jealous that most of the fortune was being taken away by the three outsiders, though he knew that they would hand it over to Roark. He felt jealous even though he tried to justify that it was fair enough because he wouldn't have made at least so much fortune without their help.

As per the plan, the brass chest of fortune and Georgina's body were left with Jacob, who brought them to his cabin with Peter and Brayan's help.

CHAPTER 13

~~~~~ 〇 ~~~~~

Jacob, Peter and Brayan arrived at Jacob's cabin on the eighth day of their expedition at sunrise. They had brought the brass chest and Georgina's body with them.

Olivia had just woken up and had her morning coffee when she heard the galloping horses approaching. She was excited to guess it was Jacob, back from his expedition. Before leaving for the journey, Jacob had informed her that he would bring his associates to the cabin if they found the treasure. As she heard clippity-clopping of many horses approaching the cabin, she became alert and scampered towards the bedroom to conceal herself.

She was overjoyed to see Jacob through the crack in the door, and her heart filled with songs experiencing a blithesome moment of light-heartedness. She was so relieved that Jacob was back. She also recognized the other two men, Peter and Brayan. She couldn't discern what exactly was happening; all the commotion outside!

The three men placed the brass chest and Georgina's corpse in the porch. They flumped on the chairs in the porch and let their hair down. 'What will be our next move?' Asked Brayan to Jacob.

'As decided, I'll keep the treasure with me and

safeguard it, till it is passed on to Roark. Today, I will also make a phone call to the middleman, Wolfe, to send a helicopter to ship the treasure to the island where Roark resides. I'll hand over Georgina's body to Glinda for performing respectable last rites,' said Jacob.

'How do I know that you two are not gonna double-cross with me?' asked Brayan.

Peter was annoyed, listening to Brayan's question. Still, he said calmly, 'Brayan, you have been one among us. We have worked together on this mission with trust and harmony. You don't have to worry about being cheated at all. You are not new to Roark's projects. Your share will be given to you by Roark. It is your second time with Roark, and you know that everything is well planned and organized in his missions. Also, we have Roark's spies over our heads, and none of us would dare to cheat the other or Roark. None of this matter, what I'm saying, is new to you. If you are uncomfortable, you can stay back here with the treasure till the helicopter arrives,' said Peter.

Brayan felt solace and said, 'No, I do not intend to stay back here. I wish I could trust you. Just that I'm a little concerned because, in my first mission with Roark, he did not remunerate me handsomely. Of course, Roark had his reasons.' he said.

'Of course, maybe Roark was not satisfied with

your work, then. But he has hired you the second time, which indicates he still believes in your potential. You have done a good job this time, and please don't mess it up by mistrust,' said Jacob.

Brayan kept silent, as some other stupid plan was taking birth in his clumsy head. The trio had some coffee and toast. Peter and Brayan took leave of Jacob, promising to wait upon him for further instructions. As soon as the two men left, Jacob came inside the bedroom and hugged Olivia.

'Oh! Jacob, I've missed you so much,' Olivia said, hugging him tighter.

He kissed her on her lips and said, 'I missed you terribly, Rose. I can't believe that I'm back here with you. Sometime during the expedition, I'd lost hopes thinking I won't be able to see you again,' he said with compassion, kissing her again. 'Come with me. I need to show you something fascinating,' he said, taking her out to the porch. Olivia was left flabbergasted upon seeing the brass chest and the body.

'Can you believe it? This is Georgina!' said Jacob, lifting Georgina's body and placing her comfortably on the couch in the living room, covering with a blanket. 'Georgina must be cold,' he said sotto voce, winking at Olivia and she laughed, delighted.

'Gracious! This is amazing,.... unbelievable!

How do you know it's none other than Georgina?' Olivia asked.

'It's her tattoo with Jett's name and the diamond necklace with the key fixed to it, as hinted by Glinda,' he justified.

The duo sat in the porch, holding each other, while Jacob recounted his ventures and about how he'd come to find the treasure and the body in a miraculous manner. He also described his divine experience at the peak of Mount Jett.

'You won't believe it. I truly felt deeply connected with Mount Jett. It was a spiritual experience, and all the miraculous things that happened eventually were truly unimaginable. It's all destiny,' he said emotionally.

Olivia chuckled. 'Jacob, you are one hell of an adventurer. I knew you would be successful in your mission. More than anything, I wanted you to come back to me at any cost, unhurt, and that was all I wished for. How I yearned and pined for you!' she said, clutching him tighter, as if she was never gonna let him go away from her again. They sat embracing each other for some time, having a moment with each other. Later, he opened the chest and showed her all the precious jewellery. She was enthralled and couldn't believe her eyes.

'This is great! So are we going to hide the treasure in the cellar at the bottom of the cabin?' she asked.

'Of course, we are,' said Jacob.

'By the way, who is this Roark, the mastermind? Is he so powerful that no one dares to cheat on him?' She asked curiously.

'I know about Roark as much as you already know and it's no use trying to find out more about him because that's not possible. Whoever he is, he is one hell of a taskmaster, who plans rackets in a very efficient way, right from his island,' said Jacob.

'True, but whoever he is, let's not worry about him. Come with me now. I need to show you something as well,' Olivia was craving to exhibit her progress with the cellar below. The two of them carried the chest to the back of the cabin. As the two went down the basement, Jacob was pleased to see the way Olivia had transformed it into a neat, cuboid, spacious basement.

'Wow! Rose, you have done a great job. It looks like you have kept yourself extremely busy when I was away on my expedition. I am very proud of you,' he extolled her, and Olivia gleamed with joy.

'Jacob, you know what? After I finished remodelling the cellar, I encountered something interesting as well. Look here, I found this metal vase,' she showed him the vase she'd located with the help of the metal detector. He studied it and said it was quite a rare piece and undoubtedly valuable.

'Not bad, Rose, you have become a detectorist,' he looked at her with admiration.

As the cellar was much more profound and broader now, an idea flashed in his head. He brought out the metal detector from the big green bag to study the cellar's walls and floor just out of curiosity; for fun.

'Jacob, I want to operate the detector. Won't you let me do it? And please show me again, how to operate it,' she requested like a child. He agreed and showed her how to use it.

As she started studying the area, Jacob was alerted by the beep emanating from the metal detector, indicating something was there underground near the pit's base on its right wall that aroused his interest. He took the metal detector from Olivia and started to examine the area thoroughly, himself. When Jacob got suspicious, he put off the machine at one spot and began to burrow at the right wall of the pit at the base. After tunnelling for about two feet in the wall sideways, he got the glimpse of another metal object.

The duo started to excavate the area, shovelling and pushing aside the mud, rocks and roots blocking the object. When they cleared the area surrounding the thing after working for nearly half an hour, they were stunned to see what it was. 'Good God! It's the golden Buddha idol!' Olivia screeched with excitement, and Jacob couldn't believe his eyes.

A couple of days earlier they had gone all the way to the mid of timberline on the north face, to locate Buddha Idol and had returned in vain. Now the idol was right here at the base of Jacob's cabin! *What a coincidence! And what a miracle! What luck!* The duo chuckled, looking at each other's' faces, amazed by another miracle. It was such a pleasant surprise! They rejoiced the moment by gazing at Buddha Idol in awe and feasting on its magnetic charisma. The idol looked magnificent, though it was soiled with mud and clay at the moment.

'Smiling Buddha idol is so beautiful, and the art is like no other! All in gold! Look at the divine sacred smile on Buddha's lips, so captivating! No wonder this idol was Jungle Jett's favourite piece of art and of course, his lucky charm!' exclaimed Olivia.

To their amazement, they also saw there were several diamond studs fixed to the golden shawl on Buddha's attire and were amazed by its star quality. Now that they had found both the brass chest and the smiling Buddha idol, Jacob thought the mission could be concluded.

'Jacob, Roark will be pleased with you, and he is going to remunerate you very well. You have done a great job, and you are going to be rich forever,' said Olivia.

'Olivia, it was you who found the Buddha idol. The credit must go to you. I will mention your efforts to Roark and see that he remunerates you equally. If it were not for you, the Buddha idol wouldn't have been found at all. If you had not excavated the remaining part of the pit, finding the idol was totally out of the question,' he justified delighted.

'Jacob, nothing else truly matters to me, more than you. As long as you are with me, I want nothing else,' she said and hugged him again. The duo kissed with compassion.

She looked at Buddha idol doubtfully and asked, 'Jacob, I wonder how the idol ended up here and not at the timberline? It was buried there at the timberline along with Jett's body, right?'

'True, Olivia, but that was something like a century ago. In these 100 years and more, Mount Jett has undoubtedly faced many natural calamities like thunderstorms, snowfall, earthquakes, landfall, avalanches, to top it up-there was an eruption of a volcano nearby on Mount pirate. I reckon, the idol somehow got misplaced to a level quite lower to its original place where it was buried underground at the timberline. As you know, the idol was buried on the North Face of Mount Jett. And my cabin is on the North face too, but, at a much lower level. Nature keeps amazing us with miracles,' he justified and tried giving a probable explanation for the appearance of Buddha idol at a different location relatively lower to where it was buried, which amazingly and coincidentally happened to be beneath Jacob's cabin.

Olivia looked at the idol in amazement and stated, 'This is fate, "the right person in the right place at the right time"!' he laughed at her own statement. They kept the locked brass chest and Buddha idol safely in the cellar among the rubble and covered with a sheet. They came out and closed the secret door and secured it again with shrubs, plants and thorny twigs.

That afternoon, Jacob went to the town and met Glinda, who was quite jubilant and stable with her health. Before he left the cabin, Olivia had pleaded him not to leave her all alone at the cabin with the treasure. He'd assured her saying she would remain safe, hopefully, with the invisible spies around, safeguarding the treasure. Still, he'd given a loaded pistol to Olivia to defend herself and had instructed her to keep her eyes open for any danger while he was away. Still, she was nervous. He'd convinced her saying it was imperative to meet Glinda; to hand over Georgina's body for performing the last rites; to bid Georgina a final farewell, wishing her soul to rest in peace.

At Glinda's shack, he narrated everything to

Glinda about their miraculously successful mission. Glinda suspired with relief to know that the mountain had revealed itself at last. She was emotionally stirred and overwhelmed to see Georgina's body. They performed Georgina's funeral the same afternoon, in a religious manner with funeral prayers and bid her final farewell. Glinda and Jacob thanked each other for everything. Glinda said that now she was free to die happily and that she felt lighthearted at the moment. She wished Jacob good luck for his future. Jacob presented the diamond necklace to Glinda, but she suggested that he keep it with him, saying it would come handy someday. Simultaneously, Glinda winked at Jacob, instructing him to take good care of the secret girl staying with him on Mount Jett. Her insights enthralled him, and he promised her he would. He bid her a fond goodbye after hugging her affectionately with happy tears in his eyes.

Jacob and Peter made a secret call to Wolfe, the middleman, to send the freight helicopter at the earliest to carry the treasure. They were promised that the helicopter would leave at the earliest and reach the cabin by next dawn. Safeguarding the treasure till the daybreak was going to be a challenging task.

~ ~ ~ ~

Back in town, Brayan and Gilbert sat snacking in a restaurant, and the duo looked crestfallen and gloomy.

'Gilbert,' said Brayan, 'somehow I'm having a terrible feeling about the whole affair. Roark hired me, like Jacob and Peter. I have been an important part of the mission all the while similar to them. But I felt left out throughout the mission and have a sick feeling that the two of them are gonna pull the wool over my eyes. I don't understand why Glinda did not give me equal importance. This is not at all fair. Gilbert, I need your help.'

'I feel resentful too,' said Gilbert. 'I'm the local man here, and I desperately feel that it is unfair for some outsiders to come and take away the whole treasure which I have been trying to get my hands on, since many years. Of course, Jacob and Peter have given me a reasonable daily wage and some measly stones and pearls, like throwing a biscuit at a dog. They have assured me that I would still be getting paid handsomely by some unknown person, the taskmaster behind this project. But who the hell is that person? And who knows if he truly exists?

With all efforts I have put in, in all these years, whatever I have been offered now is not good enough at all. I have been building a castle in the air imagining myself a rich person, once the treasure was found. Now that we have successfully bagged it together, I don't even have any hopes that at least some reasonable part of it will be mine. What if Roark is a tyrant?' he said with a worried look, though in the heart of hearts he was happy with whatever he'd got for now and whatever he was going to get from the mastermind later on, hopefully. He also knew that his contribution towards the mission was negligible compared to Jacob and Peter's. Still, greed had gotten the better of him.

Brayan tried to analyze the situation. 'Of course, we know that Jacob and Peter have done the main technical job to make it possible to reach the treasure. But that doesn't mean we have a lesser contribution. Jacob fell into a wide crevice and directly landed in front of the brass chest by a fluke of kismet. But we have accompanied them all along, risking our lives and working equally hard. They might be skilled and lucky, but we have put in all our efforts as well. They said they would hand over the treasure to some big shot who knows all about trading smuggled goods, but how can we believe in this whole affair when Glinda and the two of them have always kept us in the dark and took help from us only when they needed labourers. We are not even sure whether this whole affair will benefit us in a true sense. We cannot let them do a number on us,' said Brayan.

'We need to do something, Brayan,' said Gilbert, feeling desperate.

'Of course, we must,' said Brayan, in a determined tone. 'I have a plan, and that's why I said I need your help. If we could lay our hands on the brass chest full of fortune, ones for all, our life would be on the moon, and we don't have to struggle anymore in our lives. So this is our best chance. Let's ditch Adrian and Darby as well, as they are silly, benighted, easily quenchable village people.

I have seen Jacob's cabin as I had been there two times. The second time I went there was today morning with Peter, to drop the chest and Georgina's body at his cabin. In fact, they suggested me to stay back and help safeguard the treasure until it is consigned to Roark. But I denied as I had other plans. I do not want some stupid unknown mastermind to bag all the glory. So today morning, when we took leave of Jacob, I parted ways with Peter as well and went back closer to the cabin and watched Jacob from a hideout to see what he was going to do with the brass chest,' he said.

'Really?' exclaimed Gilbert, mesmerized. 'That's very intelligent of you. What did Jacob do with it? Where did he hide the chest? And what is your plan now?' asked Gilbert; impatient.

'I noticed something unanticipated at his cabin,' said Brayan. 'While I was watching, I saw a girl with Jacob, whom he has never introduced to me even though I have been to his cabin twice. We're here on an important undercover mission, and Jacob has a secret girlfriend with him in his cabin! Somehow, everything looks phoney. I feel that Jacob is fraudulent and has some nefarious plans with the girl and the treasure. I strongly feel he's gonna ditch us. I do not want to let that happen. So we need to act in double-quick time before it is too late,' he suggested, all determined.

'A girl?!' exclaimed Gilbert. 'Who do you think she is? Did he get his girlfriend with him to this mountain? And why did he keep her a secret from all of us? It, of course, looks fishy,' he said.

'True, definitely looks fishy and I don't know who she is,' said Brayan. Moreover, I saw that Jacob and the girl carried the brass chest towards the cabin's backyard. I was quite a distance away from them, so I could not see where they disappeared after that. I'm sure they haven't kept the chest in the cabin, instead, have hidden it somewhere behind the cabin. We need to steal it before it is sent away in the helicopter,' he said.

'What helicopter?' asked Gilbert.

'Of course, the helicopter that would be sent by Roark to carry the treasure to his island,' said Brayan. 'But I'm not sure when and where the helicopter would arrive. So before that, we need to act,' he said.

Gilbert felt anxious. 'But what about Roark's spies? What if we get hurt or even killed in the process? Everything we have done till now will become worthless and all squandered,' worried Gilbert.

'I don't believe if there are any spies. I haven't encountered even one in my last mission with Roark. We only have their word for it to keep us under control and true to the mission - I mean their mission,' said Brayan, mocking, trying to encourage Gilbert, to head-on and help him steal the chest.

The duo decided to go to the cabin straight away. Brayan called Peter on the phone casually to know his whereabouts. Peter said he was with Jacob at Penridge and that they had phoned Wolfe to send the helicopter. He also ignorantly said the helicopter was arriving the next dawn. Peter did not have the slightest idea that Brayan and Gilbert were planning to steal the chest. He even invited Brayan to join in with them at Jacob's cabin before dawn.

Brayan was happy to know that Jacob was not there in the cabin at the moment. He decided that this was the right time and opportunity to steal the chest, though he was a little worried about the girl in the cabin. He soothed himself, thinking it was only a girl and wouldn't be tough to handle if at all she posed any problem.

Deciding to leverage the moment, Brayan and Gilbert left for the cabin straight away and reached there by dusk. They watched the cabin's backyard from a distance and saw the light in the cabin, which indicated the girl was inside. They hurried towards the cabin's backyard and sneaked around to see if there was any secret place where the chest could have been hidden.

'Brayan, I think it is better if we apprehend the girl and push her to guide us to the treasure. That might make the task easier,' suggested Gilbert.

'No Gilbert, don't be hot-headed. What if she is dangerous? A girl gallantly staying alone in a cabin on a mountain with the treasure, must undoubtedly be a brave-heart,' said Brayan. 'We cannot underestimate her strength. She might even be armed. So it is better if we steal the chest in secret without her knowledge. I am sure the chest is hidden somewhere around here. Come on, hurry and look for the secret place where it could be stashed.'

Still, Gilbert peeked through the bedroom window. But, didn't see anyone. He was too curious to see the girl.

'Gilbert, instead of being curious about the girl, please concentrate on the job,' cautioned Brayan. The cabin's stilted foundation at the back was entirely covered with shrubs, herbs and thorny twigs. In the process of trying to find the secret bolthole, Gilbert got pricked by a long sharp thorn, and he squealed in pain.

'Shut up, Gilbert. Don't make any sound, its risky!' rebuked Brayan sotto voce, but Olivia, who was in the kitchen preparing dinner, heard suspicious sounds and became alert. She came out of the cabin and scanned the surrounding area. By then, Brayan and Gilbert had found the secret door at the back of the cabin, had managed to break in, into the pit at the bottom of the cabin, closing the secret door behind them.

Olivia darted to the backside of the cabin and found nothing suspicious. She thought it was her imagination due to her anxiety, felt kind of nervous and thought she would safeguard the chest, armed, till Jacob returned. So Olivia went inside, came back with the pistol that Jacob had given her and sat on a small flat-topped rock a little distance away from the secret door, lying in wait for anything dicey. She could never have guessed that there were two burglars already lurking inside the cellar. She felt edgy and brittle while she sat there, wondering where Roark's spies were!

Brayan and Gilbert scanned the cellar's interior with their torches and found many junk artefacts, rocks and metals covered with sheets and stuff. But ultimately, they were delighted to see the brass chest gloriously sitting in one corner of the pit perfectly secured with a huge lock!. They were not aware of Buddha idol, so did not try to look for it!

'Gilbert, help me lift the chest,' whispered Brayan to Gilbert, who was amusingly studying the other artefacts dumped there with the hope that he might find something else that could be valuable. 'Let's not waste anymore of our precious time. Let's hurry up now. Jacob might return anytime soon,' cautioned Brayan.

The duo carried the heavy chest upstairs and out of the cellar with great difficulty. Brayan and Gilbert had nil notion that the girl was sitting outside the secret door in the backyard, guarding the treasure.

Olivia was dumbstruck to see the two shady burglars emerging from the underground cellar out of the blue, with the brass chest in their hands. She stood up in shock and remained rooted to her spot, delirious. She soon pulled herself together and decided to protect the treasure from being stolen, though it cost her life. She knew she owed it to Jacob.

The two men jumped out of their skins when they saw the girl with a pistol in her hands. More shocked was Gilbert. But when he focused the torch on the girl, he was relieved and at the same time surprised to learn that it was none other than Olivia! He started to giggle heedlessly.

'Rose, what the hell are you doing here? Please drop the pistol,' he shouted to her. Olivia was more shocked to realize that he was Gilbert, her evil ex-boyfriend.

'I never guessed even once that the girl staying

with Jacob, could be you,' said Gilbert, still giggling and mocking her. 'I thought you went away to a far off city. How come you ended up here with Jacob, that too daringly guarding the mighty treasure like Georgina herself?' he jeeringly tee-heed.

Brayan was confused, listening to Gilbert. He was in no mood to entertain the conversation and wanted to go away from that place at the earliest. Olivia undoubtedly guessed that Gilbert was in the process of stealing the chest having joined in hands with Brayan.

Brayan said nervously, 'Gilbert, this is no time for silly talks. I don't know this girl, and we need to hurry.' He tried rushing the situation, while Olivia raised her gun at Brayan and kept shifting its direction between Brayan and Gilbert.

'I won't let you guys steal the chest. Jacob is a good person and doesn't mean to ditch you,' she tried to reason with them in a stern tone. 'You cannot cheat him by stealing the chest. Gilbert, how could you be such a putrid mug, to be doing such bad things all your life!' she cursed Gilbert. Brayan was shocked to see a determined look on her face and guessed she could shoot at them anytime if they tried to carry away the chest.

'Who the hell is she? Do you know her? She looks feisty and dangerous,' said Brayan to Gilbert, all confused, and shocked by the ominous look on her face.

'Do I know her?!' giggled Gilbert, awkwardly repeating the question. 'She is my runaway bride, my girlfriend, who escaped from me and is bitching out here with Jacob. Whoa! What a catch, Olivia!' he said derisively.

'Bite me, don't call me your girlfriend. I am not your girlfriend,... no more, I hate you. I hate your guts. You are no one to me now, and I have nothing to do with you anymore. Enough is enough. Keep the chest on the ground and scram to save your lives. Otherwise, you both will be dead in no time,' she warned.

They placed the chest reluctantly on the ground. Gilbert started to walk towards her recklessly. She panicked a little and shouted at him, 'Don't you dare come near me. I'll shoot you, you dirty scoundrel,' she lashed out at him with all her anger of the past and the present.

Gilbert mockingly tried soothing her, 'Honey, come back to me, darling. I would take good care of you with all this fortune in my possession. I know you'll come around,' he said with jeering courtesy.

'One step more and you're dead,' she shouted.

It was too much for Brayan. He somehow wanted to quit from there with the chest and implored Gilbert to come back and help him carry it.

Gilbert returned to Brayan ignoring the tiff and whispered in Brayan's ears. 'Brayan, she is a timid creature. I guarantee you that this girl is not gonna shoot because she doesn't even know how to use a toy pistol. How can she dare to use a real gun? Maybe it's not even loaded, and she is just trying to scare us. I know her. She's one faint-hearted soul!' he assured Brayan and the two men lifted the chest again. Without giving her a damn, they turned tails and sprinted towards their horses as fast as they could. Brayan mounted on his horse with the brass chest. Gilbert also mounted on his horse saying mockingly; he would come back and pick her later. The two of them trotted off.

Olivia was confused about whether to shoot or not. She had never once held a real pistol in her hand in her whole life, and she felt Gilbert was right, that she was very timid. But this time, she did not want to let go. She did not want to let Jacob down. She impulsively shot at Gilbert who was pacing behind Brayan. The bullet that emerged from her pistol directly hit Gilbert at the back of his head, and instantly he fell dead on the ground. Brayan was shocked, but he was already racing quite ahead and did not stop even to look back and disappeared with the brass chest among the clusters of spruce and pine trees, leaving Olivia in shock and despair.

Gilbert was dead, and the brass chest of treasure

was stolen. Olivia slumped on the ground in distress, sobbing with fear and disappointment. *Oh God, I've killed Gilbert. I am a killer and a loser too,.... the treasure is gone as well,... what have I done? How could I have let this happen, on my watch? I'm good for nothing. I'm just a little timid creature. What would Jacob do with me? Oh God please help me,* she murmured, bewildered.

She had never experienced such a grave situation at any time in her life before. She just couldn't suck the problem up. Jacob had informed her that the helicopter would be arriving by dawn and she felt extremely guilty that she had screwed everything up. Jacob had told her to use the pistol if necessary, but it was one hell of a bad feeling, after killing someone, that too whom she knew all these years. For a moment, she thought she should have shot Brayan as well to protect the treasure, but Olivia had been so delirious and scared then, that she'd failed in her decision making.

She had never thought she would be experiencing something so fearful and freaky anytime in her life. She did not know what to do now and how to face Jacob. She squalled, crying bitterly. She felt faint due to extreme shock and not being able to cope with the reverberations, she fell unconscious on the ground, quite a distance away from the cabin, with the pistol in her hand. Gilbert had dropped dead a few yards away from her, his body lying in the puddle of his warm blood.

CHAPTER 14

~~~~~ ☐ ~~~~~

Olivia opened her eyes to the loud, chopping sound of the helicopter. For a minute, she felt disoriented and confused. She looked around to comprehend the situation she was in. She immediately perceived that she was lying on the bed in Jacob's cabin and there as no one around her. *Whatever happened to me? And who brought me into the cabin?* She wondered, trying to recall her memories of the recent past. No sooner had she remembered Gilbert and the stolen brass chest than her stomach churned with anguish.

Where is Jacob? Is he back? Is he okay? What is that harsh earsplitting sound? Oh God! It looks like it's the helicopter! Is it daybreak? Has the helicopter arrived to fetch the treasure already? Gosh! But the brass chest is stolen, and how is Jacob gonna bear the brunt of it all? I have put him in a dire situation,... how can I forgive myself? And how can Jacob forgive me? I have let him down. I'm worthless; I couldn't even perform one fundamental task properly. I should have shot both the cheats. Why did I let Brayan take away the chest? Why didn't I act with wisdom? Olivia regretted endlessly and begged God to grant her a second chance to safeguard the treasure to get her folly corrected.

Georgina has guarded the treasure for more than 100 years till the right person came by to fetch it; I have failed to protect it even for half a day; Olivia felt sad and damned herself for being such a bubblehead.

The helicopter's pulsing noise was louder now as if it had approached right near the cabin. *Where is Jacob?* She tried to regain control of her emotions but in vain. Bestirring herself, Olivia staggered out of the cabin, still feeling physically weak and mentally confused. As she stepped on to the porch, she lightened up a bit upon seeing Jacob and Peter, who were marshalling and waving at the helicopter with a flashlight, aiding its landing. But her comfort was short-lived as she felt too guilty to show her face to Jacob because she'd messed up everything at the last minute. *I'm just a piece of shit!* Her head started to ache and felt like it was going to explode.

Still, trying to simmer down a bit, she sat on a chair in the porch and watched with anxiety as the helicopter landed on the open flat field in front of the cabin. She was awestruck looking at the stateliness of the glorious black whirlybird but was in no mood to enjoy its majestic alighting. She could not decide whether to go back into the cabin to hide or stay back there in the porch. *Gilbert is dead. So it doesn't matter whether I stay out here or conceal myself inside the cabin,* she thought wryly and stayed put. But she was apprehensive and worried about what would happen when Jacob found about the stolen chest.

Does Jacob know about the stolen treasure yet? How will he react when he is revealed of the bitter truth?! Is he going to shut me out?! She shivered by the mere thought of parting with him for good. She closed her eyes and desperately prayed to God to rectify everything and ease the situation. *Please, God! Save me, help me, protect me, support me, strengthen me,* she adjured.

She hopelessly regretted, going haywire, feeling dizzy again. As the helicopter landed on the open area, two men, in black, deplaned from it and greeted Jacob and Peter in front of the cabin. Olivia shivered as Jacob escorted all the men towards the porch after a few minutes. The cold breeze felt more prickly and brutal. Jacob was surprised to see Olivia on the patio.

'Hey Rose, are you alright? You look terrible,' he said, kneeling in front of her, holding her cheeks in his palms, looking worried. When she nodded yes, he stood up and introduced her to Peter and the other two men. They greeted her, though Peter was a little surprised to see the strange girl in Jacob's cabin out of the blue.

'Jacob, can you give me a minute? Please come on in, I need to talk to you,' Olivia said desperately, and the duo went inside the cabin while the other men waited outside. 'Jacob, I'm so sorry,' she hugged him and started to cry.

'Whatever happened to you, Olivia? What's wrong? When I returned from Glinda last night, I saw you in bed fast asleep. I did not want to disturb you. So I did not wake you up. What happened?' he held her in his arms and caressed her back. Why do you look so worried? Did anybody try to hurt you? What are you sorry about?' he asked solicitously.

'Jacob, I don't know how to explain this to you? It's so awful and shameful. Unexpectedly, Brayan and Gilbert were here yesterday at dusk to steal the chest. Trying to protect the chest, I shot Gilbert dead. But due to my inefficiency and stupidity, I let Brayan steal away the chest. I failed to stop him, Jacob. So the chest is lost now. I am a killer too, and it is because of me that all your efforts have been rendered meaningless,... I'm so sorry. I don't know what to do now?' she squirmed and sobbed.

'What are you saying, Olivia?' Jacob said bewildered. 'You mean Gilbert is dead while Brayan stole away the chest?'

'Yes, Jacob. You heard me right,' she mumbled. 'After that incident, I fainted among the pines, and I don't know who put me in the cabin. Gilbert's body must be lying somewhere in the woods a little farther away from where I'd blacked out. I am damn worried. What are you going to tell Roark's representatives who have come to fetch the chest? How are you going to justify this with Roark? What if he gets disappointed and angry with you and decides to destroy you? God! Jacob, I cannot bear it. I shouldn't have taken shelter in your cabin in the first place. I have brought you bad luck; it's all my fault,' she confessed and kept grieving.

Jacob, for a moment, looked aghast but soon recovered. Instead of being angry with her, he held her closer in his warm embrace, and the duo stood still for a moment in silence as he let her ease up slowly.

'Say something, Jacob. I can't bear your silence,' Olivia pleaded in a hushed tone. It seemed like he was looking into the vacuum, with his face drained of all the charm, mulling over the unfortunate outcome of the entire mission. She looked at his face and saw that, instead of feeling disappointed, he was trying to figure out what to do next, with the chest gone.

'Olivia, it's not your fault at all, it's mine,' he finally spoke. I shouldn't have left you all alone in the cabin, especially in a time like this. Whatever happened, has happened probably for the best. God's willing! You have done the best you could. You shot Gilbert for a good cause. So you don't have to feel guilty about that. Now relax and pull yourself together. I'm not upset with you. Come on, let's go to the cellar below and see if Buddha idol is intact at least. Maybe Roark will be happy with the Buddha idol and may decide against destroying me,' he said and slowly led her out of the cabin and moved towards the cellar door at the back of the cabin. Olivia felt comforted because she knew that Buddha idol was not stolen. Simultaneously, she was amazed by Jacob's supporting response towards her which proved he loved her truly.

Peter and the two men in black, waited for the proceedings. Jacob waved Peter to follow him to the backyard.

'But who is the girl, Jacob? You never mentioned her before,' asked Peter sotto voce, following Jacob.

'Peter, as I already introduced her to you, the girl is Olivia. Please don't ask me who Olivia is for the time being. I will tell you everything later; about who she is and how I met her. Now listen to me carefully,' said Jacob. Jacob explained the current situation to Peter and the reason why Olivia was upset.

Peter was taken aback hearing about the stolen chest, but he trusted Jacob and believed there was no trickery involved from Jacob's side.

The trio entered the cellar and scanned the area with the help of a torch, and of course, it was very disappointing to see that the brass chest of treasure was missing. Soon Jacob started to meddle with the junk spread out there searching for the Buddha idol. Most of his tools were also lying there among the rubble. He unveiled the artefacts and other wastes from one side of the cellar. He started to dig the wall where they had initially found Buddha idol.

'Jacob, you had hidden the idol among the rubble here and had covered it with a sheet, right? But where is it? Even the idol is not seen among the stuff now,' Olivia panicked. 'Why are you digging back on the wall where we originally found the Buddha idol?' she asked, curiously as if he was doing it unnecessarily.

He did not say a word, instead kept excavating the wall and moving aside the rubbish, mud and rock. Finally, they opened the hole. Olivia's eyes sparkled on seeing the Buddha idol, smiling and glowing in its original place. Peter was surprised to see it as he had no idea that they had found the Buddha idol. But something queer happened at the moment. There lay the big green tool bag beside Buddha idol in the inner excavated hole.

'Why did you hide the green bag as well? How did this huge green bag end up here? It's the tool bag, right?' Exclaimed Olivia, inquisitively.

'The green bag is here because.....' said Jacob taking the green bag out of the inner side hole, '... I kept it here,' he winked at her and asked her to unzip the bag. She slowly did as he said, expecting to see the tools. But her intuition was wrong. For a moment, her heart stopped beating, upon seeing the contents of the green bag. She was tickled pink to see that the green bag contained the treasure- all the diamonds, precious stone, pearls and the jewellery; all of Georgina's possessions glittered right there in front of her eyes. The dosh that was previously in the brass chest was now glittering with brilliance in the big green bag.

'Surprise....!' Jacob exclaimed shrugging his shoulders.

'What does this mean, Jacob?!' She whooped with delight, gifting him with a rapturous liplock while Jacob received her, enfolding her by her waist. Peter was stunned and surprised by the whole series of unexpected events. But he was relieved to see that everything had turned out to be just fine with a favourable outcome.

'This means- the chest was stolen but not the treasure! As simple as that!' Jacob laughed.

For a moment, Olivia wondered if it was just a sweet dream. She pinched herself to confirm that it was all truly happening. 'Jacob, I can't believe this! You are a genius; you have a great head on your shoulders. How and when did you manage to do this? Did the spies apprehend Brayan and got the treasure back?' she asked with great wonder and appreciation.

'Relax, Olivia, it's not like that. Before I left to meet Glinda this afternoon, I shifted all the contents of the chest into this green bag and then safely placed the idol and the bag in the side hole, "a closet in a closet" that was created when we'd initially unearthed the Buddha idol. I covered the secret hole in the secret cellar back with mud and rock and made it look like just a wall of the pit.

Somehow I could never come to trust Brayan and Gilbert from the beginning. Even Glinda had cautioned me about them. So I had to be careful because this was all my responsibility until I handed the treasure over to Roark. Just to be on the safer side, I also gave you a loaded pistol for your defence if anybody tried to hurt you. But you thought, I gave you the pistol to protect the treasure. In reality, it was for your protection and not the treasure. I'd already hedged my bets by taking care of the treasure to the nth degree, concealing it from the reach of the two vandals,' he said, gleaming proudly.

Olivia sighed with relief because the treasure was all intact, and Brayan had got fooled. 'Then what was there in the chest when Brayan stole it. The chest still appeared heavy when I saw them lift it,' she asked.

'What could there be in the chest? Of course, I filled it with mud, stones and junk,' he said.

Olivia and Peter laughed at his statement. 'I always knew that Brayan and Gilbert were nothing but trouble,' said Jacob. 'I'm truly sorry for letting you square up and confront them all alone, please pardon me,' he said dramatically. Olivia was overjoyed with the gratifying twist in the tale and was truly amazed by the turn of events.

The two men in black, Roark's representatives, helped bring back the green bag and Buddha idol into the cabin. Four more men joined them from nowhere. The men in black introduced the other four men as Roark's spies who admitted that they had brought Olivia back into the cabin after she'd blacked out. They acknowledged that they'd taken care of Gilbert's body and Brayan as well. Olivia did not probe into the matter as she was not interested in it because her confrontation with Brayan and Gilbert was a nightmare. Instead, she wanted to cherish the joyful moment with Jacob. By then, it was already time for sunrise.

Even after waiting for some time, they saw that Roark's men were not in a hurry to load the treasure into the helicopter and take off. It looked like they were still waiting for the orders.

'Jacob, when is the helicopter leaving with the treasure? Why don't you ask Roark's men?' asked Olivia.

'True, let me discuss the matter with them.' Saying so, Jacob darted out of the cabin and returned after some time.

'Olivia, there is a slight change in their plan, and we've got to decide about something important,' said Jacob. She looked at him questioningly. 'Roark's representatives were about to tell me something exciting when I went out. We have a piece of fascinating news. As per Roark's instructions, he has invited us – me, you and Peter to his mansion at his private island. The representatives were waiting for Roark's instructions to take off when they received this message to invite us,' said Jacob gleefully, and Olivia looked astonished.

'Why?' he never meets his employees, right?' asked Olivia.

'You're right. Roark is not gonna meet us, but he wants to honour us at his mansion and show his appreciation by letting us have a good time on his exotic island. It seems he is pleased with our accomplishment, and he has instructed that we travel to the island in the helicopter along with the treasure,' explained Jacob.

'This is amazing!' exclaimed Olivia, thinking, everything was beer and skittles at the moment. 'Jacob, but why me? Does Roark know about me?' she asked, confused.

'Of course, he knows about you. He has men to keep him informed about everything. I have even mentioned to Wolfe about your bravery and sincere contribution towards the treasure hunt. I have even sent him your photo, informing him about your sincere help in our project. So, Roark has invited you also to his island. You must know that, without your help, Buddha idol could not have been found. It seems, this project meant a lot to him than any of his other missions, and he is pleased with all three of us,' said Jacob.

'So, what do we do now? When are we leaving for the island then?' she asked with great excitement. Olivia was excited, not because they would be honoured by Roark, but because everything had turned out well and that she was going to the island with Jacob, to have a good time. Moreover, she was happy that her stay with Jacob had extended effortlessly. She didn't have to worry for another couple of days about her future- where she would go after this beautiful phase with Jacob.

When the chest had got stolen, Olivia was damn upset and afraid that Jacob might dump her behind, along with all his other junk. But the things had miraculously fallen in place. She thanked God heartily for protecting her and her interests by giving her a second chance.

'We have a few things to do before we leave. We need to hurry with the pending errands here,' said Jacob.

There were packages of food in the helicopter. All of them, including the representatives and the spies, had breakfast. As per Jacob's instructions, Olivia helped him pack their bags for the journey. Later, with the men's help, Jacob demolished the cabin and dumped all the junk into the pit. At the bottom of all the waste was laid, Gilbert and Brayan's dead bodies without Olivia's knowledge!

They refilled the pit with mud, stones, roots and rubble. On top, they concealed the area with grass, herbs and twigs, making it look undisturbed and untouched. All this effort was to prevent any attention from the police or the government. When Jacob was satisfied that everything looked just fine, they got on board the helicopter along with the treasure, Buddha idol and Thunder, the stallion.

Olivia looked at Buddha's smiling face, enraptured. She was confirmed that the smiling Buddha was indeed a lucky charm. She understood, why Jungle Jett was sentimentally attached with the idol and why the idol was buried along with his body by his loving wife, Georgina.

The helicopter blades started to whirl, chopping the surrounding foggy air, while the helicopter soared through the high skies with the aid of its roaring engine. It was a surreal experience for Olivia, and she imagined herself being lifted to the kingdom of heavens, a garden of delight. As they jetted over the snow-capped mountains, Jacob showed her the unprecedented summit of Mount Jett; the Spruce jungle ranges' highest peak. It was a breathtakingly touchy view. As they crossed the mountain ranges and glided over the sea, Olivia felt light like a leaf and dozed off on Jacob's shoulder, snugly clutching at his sinewy arm.

CHAPTER 15
~~~~~ ◊ ~~~~~

In the helicopter, Jacob unfolded everything to Peter about how he happened to meet Olivia in a strange way; how she'd made him a plea to provide her shelter in his cabin for a few days; how they had started to live together and gotten along well with each other; how she'd grown over him; how he had begun to trust and confide in her; how she'd partaken in the ritual in disguise and desired to contribute in the mission; how she was the cardinal fillip behind the discovery of the smiling golden Buddha idol, and how she ended up killing her ex-boyfriend Gilbert, in the process of protecting the brass chest from being stolen.

'Gee-whiz! The whole story is mind-blowing,' Peter exclaimed. 'What a coincidence... that, greedy Gilbert, who teamed up with us in the chase for treasure was Olivia's ex! Of course, it looks like he never deserved her and whatever happened to him ultimately, served him right. He reaped the fruits of what he sowed,' validated Peter.

'All we've got to do now is to wait and see what is awaiting us at Roark's private island. The whole mission has been a big adventure, full of challenges, surprises and miracles. I thoroughly enjoyed it,' said Jacob delighted.

Peter concurred, pleased that it had all been

a great experience. 'Hitherto, I've participated in many great thrilling adventures. But this particular adventure has been exceptional because it is emblazed with miracles, enchanting surprises and spirituality,' said Peter, breezily.

After several hours, they were flying over the Atlantic Ocean. Jacob gently patted Olivia on her cheeks to wake her up. 'Rose, get up, you don't want to miss this beautiful view, do you? Look at the archipelago's aerial view, the cluster of islands below! They look so tiny and amazing, perfectly embedded in the endless oceans!' said Jacob, excited.

Of course, she did not want to miss any of the fun. It was a time to cherish, a time for all the fun that she'd missed all those years. She slowly lifted her heavy eyelids and looked down at the oceans through the window and was captivated by the bird's eye view of the agglomeration of fun-sized islands, perfectly embedded in the vast blue seas. It was a picturesque scene, and she filled her eyes and mind with its beauty, holding Jacobs arm as he cuddled her, pulling her closer by her waist.

'Good heavens! It's awesome!' she felt blissed at the moment, after all the hardships and turmoil she'd gone through in her recent past.

Soon the helicopter descended towards one particular lush green island that belonged to Roark. As they neared it, they saw the magnificent view of the classy, elegant mansion surrounded by the gardens of delight. Olivia savoured its killer beauty and stateliness, open-mouthed, and exclaimed 'Whoa! It's exceptional! Out of this world! How long are we gonna stay here, Jacob?'

'I'm not sure. Maybe we'll have to stay as long as Roark wants us here. Anyway, we do not have anything else to do right now but to be footloose and fancy-free. We have all the time in the world and let's make the most and best out of it,' chuckled Jacob. Olivia smiled with merriment imagining a quality time and a fun spree that they would enjoy at the beautiful island of gaiety.

The helicopter tardily landed on the rooftop-helipad, above the manor. As the three guests disembarked from the helicopter, they received a hearty and formal welcome by Roark's personnel. The big green bag of treasure and the smiling golden Buddha idol were handed over to Roark's representatives. Olivia sighed with relief when ultimately the burden of safeguarding the treasure was perfectly released from their shoulders. The personnel who included both men and women congratulated the trio for the mission's overall success. The three guests were guided into the mansion from the terrace.

Olivia kind of felt very shy and uneasy with all the attention that was lavishly torrented upon them- this was something she'd never experienced before or in the very least, imagined of anything like it. She never knew such great honour anytime in her life. Roark's personnel's perfect etiquette carried off at the moment, made her feel like a celebrity though she knew she looked shabby at the moment. Jacob and Peter shook hands with the personnel and thanked them for the great welcoming ceremony.

The three guests were then escorted to their allotted rooms. All three guests occupied three separate rooms. Olivia's room was more of a boudoir, and she was mesmerized to see its magnanimity. Olivia was a little disappointed because she did not get to share a room with Jacob. *The crude cabin on Mount Jett was better in that sense! Maybe Roark doesn't know that there's a spark between Jacob and me. I don't know myself what that spark means. Is it a spark of romance or just a spark of friendship? How can I assume that Jacob loves me, only because he has been very kind and friendly to me and has pampered me a lot, all these days?*

Leaping on to, and lying flat on the luxurious, comfy, king-size bed, she remembered her first kiss with Jacob at the cabin during their first sunset together. It had felt so right and so meant to be! *Did he feel the same way too? Just because he said several times that he missed me and liked me, it doesn't mean he loves me. Jacob has never once uttered that he loves me. I think I'm imagining things about us. I better come out of my fantasy before I get disillusioned. Jacob may or may not be having the same feelings towards me; otherwise, he would have sought to share a room with me. Maybe he just likes me, that's all and nothing more to it.*

She tried consoling herself and decided to enjoy the stay and make the best of it, as Jacob had suggested. As long as destiny proffered her with the precious opportunity to stay with Jacob, she decided to unwind a bit. Olivia relaxed and zonked out the rest of the day. Late afternoon she relaxed in a hot tub, later enjoyed a relaxing body and mind soothing spa and then visited the manor salon to get a makeover.

In the evening, they had to get ready for a formal dinner. Olivia was worried and felt uneasy because she did not have a proper dress for the evening. She entered the walk-in wardrobe attached to the room allotted to her and was delighted to find many elegant, pricey dresses, fancy accessories and expensive rakish shoes. She selected a black trumpet dress with red embroidery, which fitted her well. She was elated and got ready gleefully with matching accessories and shoes. She applied light make up using the imported exotic cosmetics available on the dresser. After she was all set, she twirled in front of the vanity mirror and felt like a princess.

Jacob knocked on her door to escort her to the dinner table. He looked at her and admired. 'You look lovely, Rose,' he said and kissed her on her cheek. She was happy but timorous; she was not used to all the glamour and glitter. Jacob was in an evening black suit, and Olivia thought he looked great- transformed from a rough and tough cowboy to a refined gentleman. He looked so much more executive and drop-dead gorgeous in his evening suit with a killer smile and fetching brown eyes.

The dinner arrangement was excellent and appealing. Olivia wondered if Roark was going to join them for dinner. *How can I be such a loony?* She laughed to herself at her silly thought. Two men and a woman joined them for dinner along with other representatives. The older man greeted the three guests and introduced himself. 'Hello, nice to see you all. I am John, and I am Roark's big brother. Here is Jordan, our younger brother,' he said, introducing the younger man. He also introduced his wife Hailey, who gave them all an amiable smile. Olivia wondered if any of the two men was Roark.

'I'm sorry,' John continued politely. 'Roark is not here on the island now, as you know he is a very busy man and will not be able to meet you all. He has relinquished to me, the responsibility of hosting you. But he is very impressed by your success and has requested me to convey you his hearty congratulations for your accomplishments. He would like to show you his gratitude by paying you a fortune and honouring you here in the best possible way. You would be staying here on the island, in the mansion as our guests for a week and you will be honoured with all the amazing things,' he assured.

'More than anything else he is impressed by your honesty, sincerity and truthfulness towards your job. Loyalty is one thing that truly matters to him in his missions; that feature in you all has impressed him the most. That is why he has invited you to his den, which he never does, to show that he is extremely pleased with your work. This project has been exceptionally crucial for him, and he does not have words to express how happy he is with all the three of you,' elaborated John, appreciating their work lavishly.

Looking at Olivia with great admiration, he said, 'Olivia, your sincere contribution towards the mission is tremendously appreciated and noticed. Though Roark did not hire you, you have been a miracle entry into his project- a wildcard entry in a reality show,' he chuckled. 'You have been a miraculous pleasant surprise in this mission, solely responsible for retrieving the Buddha idol. Roark is still thinking how to thank you for that,' Olivia felt flattered and happily glanced at Jacob. He smiled at her, patting her back, exhibiting his happiness and appreciation for her.

John continued, 'Roark wants you all to enjoy your stay in the best possible way. Now you can have a hearty dinner and enjoy yourself for the next seven days; every arrangement has been made for the same to see to it that you have a good time on this exotic island,' saying so, he raised a toast for Roark, as well as, for the victory of the virtuous mission.

The guests enjoyed the good old wines and various anonymous exotic dishes and revelled in the lap of luxury. They enjoyed their dinner to their liver's core; they hadn't had even one decent meal in the past few days on the mountains during their adventure. The evening was well spent before they tucked themselves in, in their snugly warm beds. "Luxury thy name is Roark" was the last sentence that the tipsy Olivia mumbled in her bed before she fell asleep.

~ ~ ~ ~

The island was a self-contained utopia; a beautiful place with great grassy cliffs, hilly terrains, embellished with a myriad of verdure and surrounded by the vast blue oceans stretching to the horizons.

On the first day, Roark's personnel guided the three guests on a hiking trip and a picnic. They'd left early morning to watch the sunrise from the top of a cliff, spent the whole day out-boating, fish-ing, playing water balloons, flying kites, eating and drinking. They watched in awe, the colourful sunset across the oceans before they returned, recalling the sunsets they'd watched together on Mount Jett. Jacob and Olivia were inseparable all day long. Jacob knew he would miss her in the night; in fact, he knew both were going to miss each other. So, the whole time during their outing, Jacob never once left Olivia's side. It appeared to her that he enjoyed her company very much as well and thus she felt hopeful. At the same time, they were an amiable twosome, treated Peter like a good friend making him feel comfortable in their company.

The second day, they were given the tour of the mansion, its campuses and its gardens. The estate was amazingly majestic, mystical and glowing with richness. They were enthralled to see many beautiful paintings, stuffed animals, rare antiques and artefacts like in a museum, expensive embroidered Persian carpets, unconventional designs on the walls and roofs and many more amazing things. The grand foyer in the great hall was the centre of attraction. The mansion was no less than a palace. Its grandeur was far more than expected. Olivia missed seeing Roark, the island's owner, with a child-like curiosity.

Olivia childishly imagined that she might come face to face with Roark during their tour of the mansion and said the same thing to Jacob, while he laughed at her thought and said, 'Don't be silly, Rose, that's impossible. We don't even know how Roark looks. Even if he came face-to-face with us, how are you going to recognize him,' he teased. Olivia laughed at her stupidity.

By afternoon, Peter said he was tired and wanted to rest. So Olivia and Jacob continued their stroll through the mansion. They spent some time in the mighty library with an extensive collection of books for all age groups. They visited the stables and the paddock, where they said hi to Jacob's stallion, Thunder, who was gloriously having a good time with other horses. The gardens were trim and neatly maintained with exotic non-native flowering plants, trees and shrubs surrounding several fountains. Jacob loved the billiards room. They were also amazed to see the basement cellars, which included a huge wine room and one huge ale room with storage of many foreign wines and hot beverages and drinks. They witnessed almost all the rooms except one compartment. They were told that it was Roark's special compartment; his office, that remained locked when he was not on the island.

'Jacob, among all this grandeur, it feels kind of bland to know that Roark is not here on the island right now, during our visit,' said Olivia.

Jacob looked offended, 'Olivia, it looks like you are obsessed with seeing Roark. I feel jealous,' he said with a troubled expression.

'Come on, Jacob, it's not like that. Don't you feel curious to see Roark as well?' she asked.' He is like a myth, a Godfather. When Roark has invited us to his mansion, it's not fair if he doesn't meet us. Don't you agree with me?'

'Of course, I would like to meet him, but I am not obsessed with the idea,' he said, smiling. Olivia somehow felt good to know that Jacob felt jealous. She kissed on his lips and soothed him. The two of them laughed and went back to their rooms. Late that afternoon, they had a good swim in the luxurious swimming pool and spent their evening, drinking wine at the outdoor bar by the pool, before dinner.

During the remaining days of their stay, they made the most of it- enjoying some adventure sports, water sports and relishing great food. They also went on a cruise ship and enjoyed the sea with some sea diving; visited nearby smaller islands and had fun with the tribal people. Almost every day they visited the private gym. Most evenings were spent in the music room playing the piano, accompanied by the hosts and watching movies in the home theatre. Some afternoons they lazed around on the beach drinking beer, dosing on the sand, swimming in the sea. They talked a lot the whole time, and everything was worth it. Roark's personnel escorted them everywhere they went, making them feel safe and incredibly honoured.

Olivia felt sad; their stay on the island had soon come to an end. She wasn't worried about leaving the island but was concerned about what was her future going to be like. She wanted the clock to stop here. She felt, her life was pretty beautiful and felt blessed at the moment. She felt convinced that life was not always star crossed. She was sure that her life would be complete only with Jacob around her. By seeing Jacob and how much he enjoyed her company, she somewhere in the depth of her heart had hopes that he would ask her to go with him wherever he went after their time in the island.

The last day of their stay on the island was the most crucial one. That day they remained in the mansion as they did not have any significant plans for an outing. They received a fantastic news. The personnel informed them that Roark was on the island that day and would be meeting them individually before they left. Olivia was thrilled with this unexpected news that she was finally getting a chance to meet Roark.

'Olivia,' said Jacob, seeing her excitement, 'don't be overexcited. We are not meeting him face-to-face. His personnel informed me that he would be talking to us through a microphone, and we will hear only his voice from a speaker. We have to be grateful that we are at least getting a chance to listen to his voice.'

'Really?' Olivia was disappointed. Anyway, she soothed herself, thinking she was not allowed to expect too much and whatever honour that was offered to them till now was far more than expected and more than satisfactory.

After breakfast on the eighth day, all three guests were guided to Roark's office; his special compartment. They were politely instructed to enter in and sit in Roark's office's waiting room, until they were called in.

First, it was Jacob who went in, to meet up with Roark. Olivia couldn't resist her temptation to know what was happening inside. She was fascinated and thrilled by the fact that Roark was a myth. But now he was right there, inside, with interest to talk to his guests, himself! Thirty minutes passed by, and it felt like forever.

Jacob came out, and before Olivia could ask him what happened inside, Jacob was escorted back to his allotted room. He was not allowed to meet his other associates unless they had met Roark as well.

Anyway, Olivia felt pacified to see that, Jacob looked happy when he came out of Roark's room. It looked like he was carrying a packet with him. She wondered how handsomely Roark paid him, that Jacob seemed so happy.

Peter went in next. Olivia waited for her turn, though she was feeling impatient. Patience was inevitable at this moment. The feeling of meeting up with Roark was irresistible. Her heart was beating faster, and she could hear her palpitations. Waiting to meet Roark was a queer, tough experience, though she knew she would be meeting his voice alone and not him in person.

After like 45 minutes, Peter came out. He was carrying a similar packet, and he looked quite happy too. It looked like Roark was paying his employees very well this time or maybe it was something more than that. She wondered if he'd offered Jacob and Peter, a job in his next project, pleased with their truthfulness and loyalty. If there was another project at all, Olivia wanted to be hired as well, alongside Jacob. She had too many thoughts in her mind and couldn't guess why the two associates, Jacob and Peter, looked so happy after meeting with Roark. If Roark asked her what she wanted, she decided to ask him for one precious thing that she decided in her mind!

She sighed when at last, she was asked to go in. Being overly anxious, she felt like all her energy was draining out of her body. She piled up all her courage and entered Roark's special compartment. Of course, the room was a luxurious office chamber with three doors exiting from it; there was no one inside; she saw a couple of CC cameras fixed in different corners of the office room. She realized she would hear Roark's voice only.

Soon she heard a deep voice echoing through a speaker, 'Hello, Olivia.' She was thrilled to know that it was Roark's voice and developed goosebumps all over her body. 'I'm ROARK,.... nice to meet you, Olivia' said the voice.

'Hello, Roark, nice to meet you too,' stuttered Olivia. She did not know what to speak further, 'I mean.... nice to meet your voice too,' she said and instantly regretted for saying so because she felt it was idiotic of her to say that.

She heard Roark's voice laughing merrily. 'Congratulations and thank you for your loyal contribution in my project,' he said.

'It's my pleasure, Roark,' said Olivia formally, and waited for Roark to proceed with the conversation.

'I hadn't appointed you in my mission exactly if I'm right. But it's been a miracle that you happened to contribute a greater deal in my mission and I'm very much impressed,' said Roark. 'You won't realize how happy I am about retrieving the smiling golden Buddha!' he said in a cheerful voice.

'I'm honoured, Roark,' said Olivia, feeling all ecstatic.

'Do you want to see the glorious Buddha idol once more....I mean in his present state?' asked Roark.

'Yes, of course. I want to see him again. The beauty of the idol has enraptured me.'

Roark instructed her to enter another room through the door on her left. She did as told and saw herself stepping into a spacious, luxurious bedroom that was dark inside but ambient with exotic lightings on the false ceiling, the table lamps and a few fragrant, colourful candles burning. Soon her sight was fixed on the golden smiling Buddha idol, gloriously seated on the mantelpiece. The mantelpiece looked like it was specially designed for the virtuous Buddha idol.

'WOW!!' she exclaimed. The idol looked more beautiful, jubilant and captivating than ever as if it were meant to be here in its right place; it's home. She sat on a couch in front of the mantelpiece looking raptly at the beauty of the idol. The diamond studs on Buddha's attire glittered with all glory in the ambient lightings' effect, making her feel warm in her heart. She remembered when they had unearthed the idol from down the pit when it was all dirty and covered with wet clay.

'How do you like the idol now?' Roark asked.

'I love it! It looks magnificent! Splendid! Smiling Buddha looks like he always belonged here; he looks like he is home,' she said with admiration, wide-eyed, feasting on the idol's beauty and glory.

'That's good,' said Roark and segued, 'what kind

of a prize or a gift do you expect from me, Olivia? Do you have anything in particular in your mind that truly matters to you?... Of course, I mean.... apart from the remuneration, do you want me to do anything for you? Anything that you crave for?' Olivia thought for a while and didn't know what to say.

'Thank you for asking me that, Roark,' she said and continued to tell him what she'd decided in her mind. 'Roark, if you have any other project coming up and hiring Jacob for the same, I would be interested in being a part of the team as well because I yearn to stay with Jacob always and can be your loyal employee. Nothing truly matters to me at the moment except for Jacob's love. I love Jacob with all my heart, soul and body, and I want to be with him till my last breath. I had a great time with Jacob during my stay at his cabin on Mount Jett amidst the Spruce jungle ranges. This week of holiday with him on your island has been a time to cherish all my life. Jacob means a world to me. Thank you very much for giving me such a beautiful opportunity to be on this exotic island of yours. Now I am worried that I may have to depart from Jacob after leaving the island.

Please help me, Roark. Do something that I get the opportunity to be with Jacob for the rest of my life. I know Jacob likes me, but I don't know for sure whether he loves me as I do. Getting Jacob's love and a lifetime opportunity to stay with him would be my greatest wish. That would be the best gift you can offer me at the moment. I do not want any money or fortune in terms of wealth; I want Jacob!' she said with great sentiments and desperation.

Roark laughed at her desperate wish. 'Your wish is a very strange one. Though desperate, it's impractical and a tough one for me to fulfil. I can hire you in my next project alongside Jacob, but I cannot induce love for you in Jacob's heart. Love cannot be forced. It just happens. I definitely would have done my best to fulfil your wish somehow if I hadn't seen you in your picture sent to us. You are a beautiful creature living on this earth. You deserve the best. You deserve someone like me, not Jacob,' Roark said. This statement made by Roark came to Olivia like a bombshell. She felt offended to hear Roark underestimating Jacob and boasting about himself. She was angry with Roark and didn't know what to say. All her hopes and her respect for Roark plummeted in a second.

'It looks like you are annoyed with my statement,' said Roark. 'But you need to be more practical in your life rather than emotional. I have grown to these heights because I always think practically. Jacob is just an employee, just one straw of grass in a stack of hay. You deserve someone like me; THE KING! Will you marry me, Olivia?' Roark asked with a firm but an intense voice that made her quiver like a leaf in winter.

'What?!' what are you saying, Roark? I had great honour for you and firmly believed that you would help me with my love towards Jacob. I want to marry Jacob, not you. I adore you for your intelligence and dynamicity. But that doesn't mean I love you and want to marry you. I haven't even seen you for God's sake! I love Jacob, and he is the one just perfect for me,' she said with confidence. Olivia was now worried that Roark, being a powerful and invincible man, would pull her away from Jacob by hook or crook and twist her arm into marrying the mastermind. She shuddered with the unwelcoming thought that Roark might hurt Jacob if she rejected Roark's offer to marry Roark. Olivia wished at the moment that it was better if she'd never got a chance to meet or talk to Roark personally! She hoped it was better if she'd never come to this island!

'Ok, you cannot accept my offer because you haven't even seen me. So, If you saw me, would you change your mind? I would be glad to show myself to you if you can give me the hopes,' said Roark. She was sick with shock, not knowing what to say.

'No chance, I love Jacob and only him,' she said confidently and broke down snivelling.

Soon she heard some sounds as if someone was entering the bedroom and she turned around. She saw a dark figure, a silhouette of a man a few feet behind her in the faint lights and couldn't recognize who it was.

Slowly approaching her, the strange shadowy man said, 'Olivia, please don't cry. I'm madly in love with you. Why don't you understand that? I want you to be my life partner. I have realized that, without you, my life is incomplete. I have observed you throughout the mission, and you are the best thing that ever happened to me,' Roark said, coming towards her. He kneeled in front of her and proposed, 'Rose, will you marry me?'

'Jacob! What are you doing here?' said Olivia, looking at the man kneeling in front of her, smiling fondly. She was stunned that she was talking to Jacob all this while not knowing Roark was none other than Jacob himself!

'Of course, it's me 'THE ROARK', Olivia,' said Jacob producing a finger-ring.

'You mean.... Roark is none other than my dear Jacob?!' said Olivia, fascinated.

'Yes, you are right,' confirmed Jacob, chuckling. Do you still want to marry Jacob and not me?' asked Jacob alias Roark.

'Of course, I want to marry you! YES! YES! YES! YES!' Said Olivia, her heart still thudding with excitement, not being able to digest the reality. Jacob put her the finger ring, stood up and held her in his arms, and the duo kissed passionately.

'Of course, you are right,' said some other voice coming into the room. Olivia turned towards the second voice, shivering with excitement. She saw that the voice belonged to John, Roark's big-brother- meaning, Jacob's brother. Jordan also entered the room, and the two brothers said, 'Your wish is granted, Olivia, your prize is fixed.' Jacob feasted his eyes, watching her excitement.

All this was too much happiness for her to bear. 'Jacob, is it all real?' asked Olivia, hugging him tightly with tears of joy in her eyes. 'Of course, I want to marry Jacob! I mean ROARK! I do! It is my dream come true!' she laughed delighted.

Everyone in the room clapped, congratulated the couple, wished them good luck and went out leaving them alone to rejoice the moment.

'Jacob, how could you do this to me? You are brutal!' she said, faking anger, hitting him with her fist on his shoulder.

'What have I done? I have granted you what you asked for, I mean, what you wished for!' he said trying to justify, 'and of course, I have fallen head over heels in love with you. I have swooned over you and been in seventh heaven from the day I saw you first in the lake on Mount Jett,' he finally admitted. And before she could say anything further, he locked her quivering pink lips with his hot, moist, sensuous lips. He carried her on to his gorgeous heavenly bed, and the two made love for the first time. God had been more than liberal to her in granting her wishes and protecting her interests.

'Our merger is destiny. It is decided in the heavens, I love you, Rose, more than anything in this world and it's true,' Jacob whispered lovingly, nuzzling at her ears pushing her into ecstasy with his harsh warm breath, stroking the side of her neck. At the moment, she felt her life had completely turned around and was all beer and skittles, as she lay naked, sweating and spent in Jacob's cuddly embrace, the duo chuckling and giggling in pleasure.

'How did you manage all this drama, Jacob?' she asked, her heart filling with wonder.

'Of course, it was all scripted by me,' said Jacob. 'After we found the treasure and Buddha idol, I took my family, my representatives and my personnel into my confidence to give you a big surprise of your life,' he explained.

'This is not fair, you made a fool out of me,' she started hitting him again, feigning anger, looking cross and simultaneously laughing and giggling to her heart's content.

'And why yourself and Peter looked so happy after meeting Roark? And what was there in the packets you guys were carrying when you came out?'

'That was part of the drama too. The packages just contained gift hampers, that's all. When Peter was here in my office today, I introduced myself to Peter as "The Roark", and he was extremely happy and surprised. I explained to him about my plans for you and us. I requested him to be my business partner and adviser, bowing to his loyalty. I also took him into my confidence in this act of giving you a surprise. He is amazed by our story and is truly happy for us. I am delighted that Peter accepted my offer and agreed to stay back here on my island, with us forever, as my special adviser. As simple as that!' he shrugged.

'Of course, everything is as simple as that for you,' she teased him, kissing him again. 'And I won't ask you how you came back to your office bedroom here from your allotted room just a few minutes back. I know there must be some secret passage between the two rooms,' she answered her own question and smiled. Her hypothesis was, of course, right.

In the evening, Jacob gave her the news about Glinda's demise, which had happened two days earlier, and Olivia became emotional and overwhelmed hearing about it, and her eyes welled with tears.

He also took Olivia into another room attached to his office. It was a spacious hall with many big portraits fixed on the walls. Olivia looked at the pictures with curiosity.

'Who are all these people in the portraits, Jacob? She asked.

'I brought you here into this hall to introduce you to my parents, who died a couple of years back,' he said. They moved from one painting to another, and he introduced her to the portraits of his mother and father.

He also showed the portraits of his grandparents, great grandparents and great-great-grandparents, in fact, all his ancestors from the past three to four generations.

Finally, he stood in front of a portrait of a woman in her old age. 'This is my great-great-grandmother, Cindy,' he introduced, and Olivia saw the literature written below the picture as "CINDY" {1875—1940},

'Okay....' Olivia said, keenly looking at Cindy's portrait. 'What about Cindy, Jacob? You look thoughtful. It looks like you want to tell me something about her,' reminded Olivia.

'Of course, I want to, because she is a special person responsible for all the twist of events in my life,' he said, opening the envelope given by Glinda, the old witch; pulled out a small photo from it, and handed it over to Olivia. Olivia studied the image in her hand. It was an old photo of a young woman in black and white. Olivia couldn't identify who it was. She flipped the picture back and saw the name written on it. It said, "CYNTHIA".

'Jacob, Cynthia is Jungle Jett and Georgina's only daughter, right?

Jacob took the photo from her hand and said, 'Yes, this photo was given to me by Glinda after the ritual, asking me to open it only after finding the treasure. This young woman in the photo is Cynthia. She was the only daughter of the burglar couple, Jungle Jett and Georgina who lived in the mid and late 19th century. As you know Cynthia left the mountain and went to a far off land with her husband after her father's death, while her mother Georgina stayed back at Glinda's.' Then he showed Cindy's portrait on the wall and asked Olivia to compare the two. Olivia observed the two pictures, and her heart skipped a beat.

'Oh my God, Jacob! It looks like the lady in the picture and the portrait are the same! But the one in the portrait is Cindy, and the one in this photo is Cynthia. So you mean Cindy is none other than Cynthia? And she is your great-great-grandmother?!' Olivia exclaimed.

'Exactly, you guessed it right. According to Glinda's information, Cynthia had changed her name after she'd left the mountains. She'd changed her name to Cindy.

'Wow, Jacob, this is an amazing coincidence!

You mean you are the great-great-great-grandson of Jungle Jett and Georgina! So their wealth legally belongs to you. That is what Glinda meant when she said you are the right person to reveal the mountain,' Olivia was dumbstruck with the whole twists and turns of events.

'Exactly, I guess. But until I opened the envelope and saw Cynthia's picture, I was not aware of this connection. I kept wondering why Glinda considered me the rightful person; kept wondering why I felt close-knit with Georgina's spirit and why I felt at home on Mount Jett's peak! Now I know the answers. It was all meant to be,' said Jacob. 'Maybe Glinda acknowledged me with her powers and visions. I happened to plan this mission casually, but somehow I got emotionally involved with this chase and felt connected with Mount Jett, throughout. This mission turned out to be a special one. It was, of course, a tough, challenging adventure, but I got my inheritance, and I miraculously got you. In all of my projects, I hire employees. But in this mission, I coincidently ventured myself for some unknown force that drew me into it, and I was determined not to take any chances of losing this opportunity,' Jacob said, overwhelmed.

Olivia placed her palm on his chest and sighed a big sigh of relief. 'Jacob, this is all more than amazing, but this is all too much for me to digest, I need to rest a bit,' she said, and Jacob saw that her face was glowing with happiness at the unexpected pleasant surprises. Jacob embraced Olivia, and she placed her head on his chest.

'After all, destiny has decreed triumph for me, uniting me with you and my inheritance,' said Jacob, contented.

Olivia chuckled and said, 'Jungle Jett was a skilled burglar of his times. And you, his 'three-times-great' grandson is a skilled taskmaster of the current modern times. "LIKE GRANDFATHER, LIKE GRANDSON", she stated humorously. 'Or maybe you were Jungle Jett yourself in your previous birth. You never know!!' she said while Jacob looked at her, enthralled by her statement. The duo went out of the hall, laughing aloud and holding each other's backs.

~ ~ ~ ~

After several days, Adrian and Darby received a package each, a handsome share in the treasure for their sincere help and loyalty. Back on Mount Jett, a void stood in place of Jacob's secluded cabin, as if no shady affairs had ever taken place out there on the Spruce-Jungle ranges. The caves' entrance on the east face got occluded back again within a few days, hiding the caves from the outside world forever and ever.

~~~~~◻ **THE END** ◻~~~~~

BOOKS BY THIS AUTHOR

"Mystic Souls Of The Spider-Triangle" - A Fascinating Mystery

When her good friends Steve and Robert become the latest victims of the Blackrock crossroad accidents, Zara Derek, a nineteen-year-old, amateur investigative journalist is determined to get to the bottom of the mystery. Zara is already intrigued by her own paranormal experiences and the "hauntings" which are allegedly responsible for the several accidents at the same site in the past year.

As she begins exploring the woods near the Blackrock crossroad with the help of her boyfriend, John, and his school buddy, George, they stumble upon the Spider Triangle with its convoluted, mysterious trails and uncover an eerie web of horrifying occurrences that challenge their very sanity.

Can they believe their eyes? Does the supernatural really exist? Will Zara and her intrepid friends get to the heart of this horror mystery against all odds?

Made in the USA
Middletown, DE
26 February 2021